It's All Coming Back To Me Now

Lovely Whitmore

IT'S ALL COMING BACK TO ME NOW

ISBN 9781470039806

Acknowledgements:

I have to thank my family, my children, Kashela, Kashayla, and Jekeveus, you are the reason I breathe! To my sister Shaquita, you are the best friend a girl can have! To Swa Kay for all the days and nights twelve years ago you read and reread and kept me motivated. To my dear friends, Jennifer and Armentha, who was there when I first started writing this book sitting in Job Corps goofing off with nothing else to do, thank you for giving me that motivation. Mary you read every page back then and kept me inspired! A special thank you to John for staying up with me late at night, reading over every chapter, correcting my grammar, putting up with me when I had those anxiety attacks and just wanted to write and write and write.

I love you all, hope you enjoy the book, if it wasn't for you this would have never been finished.

Latrease Wilson slung the phone down on the receiver. "The fucking nerve!" She stood up, blew the fire out of the candles, grabbed her purse and keys, and was out the door. In less than five minutes she was backing her blue 1998 Honda Accord out of the driveway and pulling out of the apartment complex. She was mad! No, she was furious! This was the last straw!

Randy had broken her heart too many times and she was not going to keep letting him do this to her! How could he be so insensitive? Just because he was older than her did not give him the right to treat her this way! This was going to be the night she would give Randy the ultimatum. Either they were going to have a relationship, a committed relationship, or nothing at all! This was the night she would finally put her foot down. She needed to know how he truly felt about her. She needed to know that their feelings were mutual.

Randy had told her when they first met that he wasn't looking for anything serious. Latrease respected that. That was a year ago and now she needed to know that they were not still on that same level. She needed assurance that this was not just a "fling"! A fling that lasted a whole year!

Every time she would get close he would only back away further. He would tell her that he wasn't ready, and that he didn't want to hurt her. She'd been hurt before. He knew that. This was not her first time being in a relationship but it *was* her first time with an older man. All the guys she dated before were her age but they were so immature. Randy was ten years older than her.

Randy had plenty of female friends; he would tell her that he wasn't ready to settle down. She had tried to act like it didn't bother her. She tried to make it seem that it didn't matter if he didn't exactly consider her his woman. She knew the truth. She knew that on those nights when he would come make love to her it was more than just sex. Well at least on her part.

Latrease turned the volume up on the CD player. She was listening to Whitney Houston, *Where Do Broken Hearts Go*; she turned the volume all the way up. Her eyes were filled with tears and it hurt to swallow.

How could he not call? How could he just not show up? How could he not even answer when she called? She knew Randy had moments when he would shut down and pull away but he had promised he would be there tonight. She had even called to make sure he hadn't forgotten or made other plans well in advance that day. He had promised! How could he intentionally leave her hanging like that? How could Randy do this after a whole year! One whole year of them seeing each other!

Latrease had been so excited about this night. She had spent 3 hours at the salon getting pampered. She had gotten her nails manicured, a pedicure and a facial. She had gotten a bikini wax. She'd cooked the most romantic meal. She had planned the most romantic evening filled with food, wine, dancing and cuddling. She wanted tonight to be perfect.

She had bought a beautiful black gown with a long split on the side that came up to her thigh. It was nice and elegant. She was wearing five inch jewel trimmed pumps with a sparkling diamond choke.

She'd even decorated the living room

a bit to set the mood. She'd spent over three hundred dollars preparing for this night. This special night. This romantic night with the man she loved. She sang along with the CD.

The song was making things worse, Latrease knew it but she couldn't turn it off. Music was her outlet. Music was how she expressed herself. She loved singing and she loved sad love songs. Plus this song was of one of her favorite artists. She'd grown up listening to Whitney Houston. Latrease knew if she didn't turn the CD off it would cause her to start hating this song. So she reached down to grab her CD case from under the seat.

She was flying down 95 South. She didn't know where she was going she just wanted to get out of that apartment. Away from that scene. Away from all those reminders of Randy. How could he not show up?

She grabbed another CD from the case. It was that of another of her favorites.

Celine Dion, *All By Myself*

Latrease was so wrapped up in her

thoughts that she hadn't been paying attention to how many miles she'd driven out of the city. She didn't recognize anything and the nearest exit sign read five miles until the next motel.

She was so tired her eyelids felt like they were trying to lift five pound weights. She didn't have any strength to keep driving.

It was late, she glanced at her watch. After 1am in the morning. She was so tired and sleepy and didn't feel like trying to drive all the way back home to her empty apartment. It would only remind her of the humiliating night she had waited so long for.

The nerve of him, he didn't even call. He just stood her up coldheartedly, like it didn't matter. Like her feelings didn't matter. Like he just plain out didn't give a damn. She'd already told him that she had something important to discuss with him. How could he be so heartless?

Latrease decided at that very moment that it was time to really leave Randy alone. If he couldn't at least call and say he wasn't coming, after one whole year of them knowing each other, spending time with each other, sleeping together, then he wasn't worth her wasting another minute thinking about!

She was singing and crying and yelling and sobbing. One more mile to go, she read off the highway sign. She couldn't control the burn in her throat, and the ache in her belly was getting more intense. She was so sleepy and tired all she could think about was a nice warm bed with a soft pillow. She thought about her parents. This had been the same road, the same exact road…

***

Thirty one year old Randy Jackson pressed the button on his garage door remote to close it after backing out of the drive way. BEEP BEEP BEEP he heard his pager go off. He had just finished taking a shower and shaving. He'd put on a pair of slacks, a light blue button down dress shirt and dress shoes since he didn't know exactly where he and Latrease were going he didn't want to be over or underdressed. Earlier he had went by the florist and bought a nice bouquet of mixed flowers with a vase and a teddy bear.

He knew how much Latrease loved those sentimental things and he knew how much this night meant to her. Something about that girl that brought out the best in him!

She had been very straight forward with him the last time they were together, almost demanding that he decide to either commit or she was going to start dating other guys. In a weird kind of way that demanding side of her turned him on. He just wasn't sure he was ready to settle down yet. She was so young and had her whole life ahead of her.

BEEP BEEP BEEP Randy reached into the glove box and grabbed his pager. He assumed that it was Latrease calling to remind him of their date. That was the one thing he didn't like about her. He didn't like to feel tied down. Even though Latrease was a nice girl as well as the closest thing to a relationship to him, he vowed that he would not go that route. It was too risky. He valued their friendship more than anything and he did not want to mess that up. He knew that he shouldn't have been intimate with her. He knew that it made things worse. But he couldn't help himself. She was so beautiful, so tender, and so young. She was twenty one, barely old enough to buy alcohol. He was ten years older than her. What could they possibly have in common? She needed to be with someone more compatible with her. Someone her own age. Not some playboy that wasn't ready to settle down.

That's why he had decided to be more distant from her the past few weeks. In hopes that she would start seeing someone else, find her Mr. Right. He just knew that it wasn't him.

"Valerie!"

Now what does she want? He thought to himself as he pulled out of Honey Grove Circle. He decided he would just swing by there since he was already in the area. Besides he still had thirty minutes before his eight o'clock date with Latrease. The moment he turned onto Valerie's street he realized that her car was not in the yard. A slight chill went through his stomach as he parked the car and ran up the hill to the porch. He started to knock on the door but he saw a piece of yellow paper sticking up out of the screen door. He pulled it out and read Valeries' scribbled handwriting. It said that Keyon (his son) had an asthma attack and she had taken him to the hospital. He ran down the steps with the letter in his hand, jumped into his car and was on his way to the hospital.

***

Valerie sat nervously and impatiently waiting for Dr. Greg Parker to return. It had been an hour since they arrived and Dr. Parker promised he'd come and update her as soon as he could. It was now almost eight thirty and he hadn't come back yet, and Randy hadn't shown up at all. Where was he? She wondered. How could he have not returned her pages? Maybe she dialed the wrong number. She decided to page him again. As she reached down into her wallet for change Randy walked in looking very relieved. "I've been to three hospitals in the past hour trying to find you. You could have been a little bit more specific." He yelled as he looked down at her. "How is he, is he alright?" he asked. "Dr. Parker is in there with him now; he should be out any minute to talk to us."

Randy then took a seat facing her. He

could sense that she was upset with him. She always was, so that wasn't new to him. She was being very quiet. He assumed that it was better that he not ask her anything to avoid an argument and that it was the last thing he wanted to do, was to argue with this woman. They had made an agreement to have a very business-like relationship. He would write her a check every month and she would call him whenever she needed something for Keyon. He would see him on the weekends that he didn't have to work or if Valerie hadn't already made plans for him.

Randy was very satisfied with the arrangements that were made. He sometimes felt a little bad that he wasn't a part of his sons' life the way he wanted to be but he was just so busy. Not only was he a therapist, but he also owned a workout gym. That took a lot of his energy and most of his time. Valerie was married and stable. She was a medical transcriptionist and did her work at home. Her husband was a karate instructor down at the local boys club. They were happy together and he felt his son was better off in a home with two loving parents that were planning to be together forever, or at least a long time.

After what seemed like hours of sitting in silence Dr. Parker returned, "Mr. and Mrs. Smith?" he asked. Randy quickly corrected him. Dr. Parker then said "Your son suffered a mild asthma attack associated with a severe bronchiolitis infection. We have not been able to determine if it is an extension of an upper respiratory infection or by a bacterial infection. He also had a fever which we have given him Tylenol and it went down. Mom, has he been coughing up any mucus?"

"Yes but I thought it was a part of his cold. I didn't know he had bronchi…bronchy…well whatever you just said. Isn't that something you get if you smoke?" Dr. Parker scribbled a few notes on his clipboard and looked at Valerie. "There are several ways that one can get bronchitis, he could have been around and excessive amount of dust or pollen. You don't necessarily have to be a smoker or around a lot of smoke. We have done some x-rays of his lungs to see if there was any fluid in them. They were fine but we would like to keep him overnight to monitor his breathing. Do either of you have any questions?" Dr. Parker looked at them both as they nodded their heads. Then Valerie asked if they could see him. He told them to follow him. They did.

Four year old Keyon Jackson lay helplessly on the bed. He was under a breathing mask that Dr. Parker had explained would give him fresh oxygen to help with the regularity of his breathing. Keyon was asleep and Valerie knew that he had to be very tired, because she was tired and they had spent the day at the zoo. That's where he had been exposed to all that pollen and dust she assumed. She told Randy that she would stay overnight with Keyon but he insisted that she went home to get some rest. He volunteered to stay there with Keyon and she couldn't do anything but agreed to leave because she was indeed very tired.

Randy spent the rest of the night by his son's side watching him sleep.

***

Beep! Beep! Beep! Randy woke up to the sound of his pager. Who in the world would be paging him at this time of the morning? He reached over to get his bag which was on the floor, and took out the pager. No number! Randy was furious! Why would someone page him this early in the morning and not even leave a number? It was three o'clock in the morning for heaven's sake!

Randy stood up from the chair and stretched. He then walked down to the waiting room and grabbed a Jet Magazine from the rack. It was a February issue and one of his favorite magazines to read. He sat in the waiting room for a few minutes and started reading the magazine. He read a few articles about some celebrities who had tied the knot then turned to the center of the book to see who was featured as centerfold of the month. "They put anybody in these books nowadays" he thought to himself as he laughed at the unattractive woman on the page. He skimmed to through the rest of the book then saw a girl that looked just like Latrease.

Latrease! "Awe SHIT!" he said to himself but it came out loud. He had forgotten all about her. He should have called and let her know what had happened. "How could I forget?" he asked himself as he looked down to his waist to get the time but realized he had left his pager in his sons' room. "Maybe she's still awake" he thought as he rushed back to the boys room. It was worth a try, for he knew that at least this time he had a good excuse. He took his pager out of the duffle bag. Someone had paged him because the light was flashing. He then looked at the number. He didn't recognize it. Who could it be he wondered as he pulled up a chair next to where the telephone in the room was? He dialed the number and it was answered after the first ring.

"Valdosta Police Department this is Detective Jennifer Wade speaking, may I help you?" surprised Randy looked at the number again and wondered if he had made a mistake or something. "Ma'am I'm sorry I dialed the wrong …" before he could finish the detective interrupted. "Is this R.J. she asked?"

"Yes, but I don't understand why the Valdosta Police would be calling me." He waited for her reply. "Is R.J. your real name?"She asked.

"No its Dr Jackson," Randy was not sure where the Detective was going with this line of questions.

"Well Dr Jackson, what is your relationship with Latrease Wilson?" she asked hoping that he would be cooperative being that she didn't really have just cause to ask him anything.

Not knowing the best way to answer the question he shot back, "Miss Wilson is my patient, what's the matter, is she in trouble?"

Detective Wade sighed before she continued, "Latrease has been in an accident, her car ran off a cliff, the hospital tested her blood for alcohol and found nothing. Your number was the last one dialed from her car phone it was around one o'clock this morning. We assume that the accident took place a little afterwards."

A panicky Randy then asked, "Is she alright, she did make it, didn't she?"

"Calm down Dr Jackson I think she will be fine she had a few cuts and scrapes, she's at the Emergency Room at Hawervan Hospital here in Valdosta. You can talk to them about her condition."

Randy sighed. He was glad to hear that she was alright.

"When was the last time you saw her doctor? I mean in your office of course?"

Do you have any idea why she would be driving down here at that time of night? Her license says she is an Atlanta resident."

He knew where she was going with this line of questioning. "She never mentioned any relatives in that area, what is the name of that hospital again?"

After another ten minutes the call ended. Detective Wade concluded that with the information that Miss Wilsons therapist had given her she could very well close the case. He had just seen her two days ago and she said that she wasn't having any stress related problems so the Detective concluded that it was just that, an accident. She then closed the case.

***

Later on that day after taking his son home to Valerie, Randy headed to his home to take a shower and put on some clean clothes. Afterwards he called Hawervan Hospital and asked to speak with the doctor or nurse that was on duty. She then told him that Latrease had slipped into a coma through the course of the morning.

"Her vitals are good and she isn't running a fever, I believe that her unconsciousness is a result of the horrifying shock of the accident. Miraculously she didn't get any major scars and there was no harm done to her unborn fetus. We do believe that she will gain consciousness soon, but with these things we can never be sure. We just have to wait it out and hope that she pulls through."

Randy was so stunned, words could not exit his mouth. There were so many images flashing through his mind. Latrease was too young to be going through all this drama. It's not fair, Randy bawled to himself as he struggled to keep a straight face. He told Dr Harmon that he would be there shortly and ended the call after giving her his pager and cell phone number in case anything happened before he arrived, being that Valdosta was an hour and a half drive away.

For a few minutes he sat and thought to himself. What was Latrease doing in Valdosta, he wondered? He couldn't help but feel responsible for what happened to her. If only he had called, he thought, and then she wouldn't be out driving in the middle of the night. She had told him that she wanted to talk to him about something important. It must have been the baby. He wanted to see her, no he *needed* to see her, to be there for her. He was all she had. The only family she had. Her parents had died a year ago in a car accident. She was an only child and she had no other relatives in the state of Georgia. She had moved to Atlanta from Macon to get away from the bad memories of her past. Randy was all she had. He knew that and that was why their friendship was so delicate to him. He knew he shouldn't have been intimate with her. He should have been more responsible…and now she was pregnant with his child, lying in a hospital bed in a coma, all because of him!

He placed one more call before he left.

"Talk to me!" a teenage boy answered the other end.

"Is that how you answer the phone at an established place of business?" Randy asked not sure which one of his nephews was on the other end.

"Yeah when my uncle owns the place!" the boy said and Randy recognized the voice.

"Kevin! You'd better learn some telephone manners before you be out of a job! Blood or no blood! You never know who could be on the other end of that line!"

"Lighten up Unk I knew it was you, why you have to be so strict all the time, can't a brotha have a little fun sometimes?"

Randy took a deep breath then firmly said, "No! Not when you are on the clock, you can't! Now put your dad on the line."

Kevin didn't respond, Randy heard his nephew put the phone down a little too hard, and a moment later Bernard was on the line. Randy told his brother that he needed him to watch the place for a couple days.

"I'm going to need the boys to do a little work for me later so don't let them wonder off too far."

"OK" Bernard agreed that he would handle the gym and keep his twin sons around until Randy called back with more instructions.

A little after four o'clock that afternoon Randy was pulling up at the Hawervan Hospital's visitors parking lot. After circling the lot several times he finally found a spot that wasn't too far away from the elevator that led to an entrance to the building.

Inside he was given instructions to Latreases' room and was asked to sign a visitor's form. He then entered the room which she shared with another woman who was watching television. At first sight of her he felt a sharp pain in the pit of his stomach. She was so beautiful, even though she was laying there trapped inside a dream that he wish she'd awaken. Her long curly dark brown hair was thrown against the pillow. Although her eyes were closed he could imagine them staring at him with that look of innocence she always depicted. Even though she was wearing a hospital gown he could see her womanly shape underneath it. She was so pretty, and attractive. He knew that he shouldn't be looking at her this way but he couldn't help himself, she was so beautiful.

He wondered how far along was her pregnancy. She didn't look it at all, he knew that for sure. He placed his hand on her stomach slightly and wondered what she'd look like a couple months from now. He wanted to be there for her every minute of her pregnancy. He wasn't able to share that closeness with Valerie and he wanted to be close to this baby. He didn't for one minute doubt that this was his baby, for he knew that Latrease was so in love with him. She wasn't seeing anyone else and to be honest he wasn't either. Sure he had occasional one night stands he was so accustomed to the love making they made. He was comfortable; she was so pure, so sweet and so innocent.

Dammit! He cursed! This was not right! He should not have been intimate with her and now he had ruined the rest of her life by making her pregnant. How could he have been so selfish? He had used protection with all the others, why not Latrease? Why was she so special? He knew the answer but just didn't want to admit it to himself. The truth was that he loved her more than he was willing to admit. More than he wanted to. He couldn't help it. He had grown so close to her that it was getting hard for him to pull away. But he had to!

Pull yourself together, he told himself. Then he left her room to find a nurse. When he did he asked if it was possible for Latrease to get a private room. The nurse told him that it would be fifty dollars a day and that in Latreases' condition she didn't know how long she would need it.

"I'll take it!" he told her.

Without anything further he took out his check book and signed a check to the hospital. He told the nurse that he would be leaving and asked, "Will she be in her new room by the end of the day?"

She assured him that she would see to it herself. He went back into the room, kissed Latrease on the cheek and left the hospital.

***

The next two days went by very slowly. He had gotten a room at the nearest hotel to the hospital. Occasionally he called Valerie to check on his sons' condition. He called his secretary and told her to reschedule all the Monday through Thursday appointments.

"Is everything alright" his worried secretary asked. Armentha had been working for him the past two years at his office. Out of those two years he had NEVER taken a day off. She wondered if something was wrong. He assured her that everything was fine and that a close friend had been in an accident. She did what he asked.

On Monday morning he went to the hospital to sit with her once again. They had just given her a sponge bath and put her on one of the new gowns he'd bought and given to the nurse. He couldn't stand the sight of those ugly cotton gowns the hospital supplied. He wanted her to at least look comfortable, even though she was sleeping away in dreamland. He grabbed her hand and wondered what she was dreaming about. Was he a part of those dreams? She was beautiful, her peanut butter tanned skinned was smooth and creamy just like it looked. As he watched her sleep he wondered if he kissed her would she awake.

Knowing in his head that it wouldn't work, he kissed her on the lips anyway. A slight smile stretched across her face. It made his day. He knew that it was probably an involuntary gesture but in his mind he felt that she was responding to him. He held on to her hand a little tighter. He didn't really know if the brief smile was real or if he imagined it. He whispered sweet endearing words to her. He knew she couldn't hear him because Dr Harmon had said so, but he wondered if maybe she could. He told her that if she would just come back that he would promise to take care of her and their child. He asked her to please come back and speak to him or at least try. He was in tears now for he feared that she may never come back. He wished that he could go back in time. he wanted to change the things he'd said to her the many times that she'd told him that she loved him. He wanted to show her so much that the feeling was very mutual. How could he have been so dumb? He knew what he felt and he knew what he wanted, and it was her. He closed his eyes and whispered a prayer.

Then he slowly opened his eyes. Latrease's eyes were opened. She was staring up at him lazily. He blinked twice just to see if this was really happening.

"Thank you Lord!" he said out loud, then opened his eyes again. She was awake, looking at him. He pushed the button on the side of her bed to get the nurses attention. Then he spoke to her.

"Hello Latrease." He said. Before he could say anything else the nurse rushed in. He told her that she had gained consciousness and that she had smiled at him a few minutes back.

Dr Harmon entered the room and asked Randy to step out. This was normal procedure so he left without any protest. She then walked over to Latrease and said, "Hello Latrease, I am Doctor Latoyya

Harmon. I know that it is going to be difficult for you to speak, because of the tube that is down your throat, but if you can hear me would you blink twice?"

After a few seconds, Latrease responded.

Dr Harmon said, "Good! Now I am going to touch your left arm if you feel it blink again." She did.

A few hours later the tube had been taken out of her throat and all but her IV had been taken out. She was no longer hooked up to the machine that was monitoring her heart. Dr Harmon had talked to her a bit more and given her a few more tests. She stepped out of the room and spoke to Randy.

"She doesn't remember anything about the accident, which is normal I expected that. She did however answer to her name and was able to verify her birthday. We did an ultrasound and the baby is fine. When I mentioned it to her she gave me a rather blank look, like she didn't know what I was talking about at all. I don't think she remembers or ever knew that she was pregnant. Well anyway, I felt that you would be the best one to talk to her since you already know her and have a relationship with her. She'll probably respond to you better about the personal things being that I am a total stranger, and besides this is your field of expertise." With that Dr Harmon exited the room leaving him alone with Latrease.

Randy frowned, he wasn't her doctor; he was her lover. In the past he had a hard time trying to get in her head. It took him months to get her to open up and talk about her parent's death. It was hard for him to get her to talk about deep things. Although this was the field that he was amongst the best in, he was not good and working with those that were close to him.

He walked over to the bed, "Hello Latrease, how are you feeling?" He greeted.

"Fine although my throat is a little sore and my back hurts. I feel like I have been laying here forever!"

"Well it hasn't been forever," he assured her. "But you have been sleeping for a couple of days."

He then decided to bring up the

subject that Dr Harmon thought she'd forgotten. "Do you remember what you wanted to talk to me about the other night?"He asked her hoping that she would remember.

"No! I don't know what you're talking about! Do I know you?"She asked wondering with a blank look on her face.

Randy watched her expressions change as he waited for her to answer.

"You really don't know me?" he asked.

"Dr Harmon said that you were my psychiatrist but I don't understand why I would need one. I'm not crazy! Furthermore I don't remember ever seeing you before!"She snapped back.

"NEVER?" he asked to give her a little time to think before answering.

He had studied a condition that he'd known about called Antiach Mind Defieincy it is triggered when a person is put into shock while already suffering stress and depression. It allows the persons mind to suppress whatever it is that was stressing them before the shock. Basically it allows the person to maintain their life in its normality with a slight case of Amnesia about what triggered it in the first place. In some cases the vague memory never came back. In a lot of them though, it did. But the one thing about it was that people around the patient were warned not to tell them about those missing pieces it would only cause their mind to block it back even further. They had to remember on their own that was the best way.

"I told you the first time; is there something wrong with your hearing?" She asked being sarcastic. "You look kind of disappointed" she paused. "Do you always get mad if your patients don't see you as their top priority?" He was cute she thought but not her type. He was too arrogant. He looked like the type that used his looks to get what he wanted. He was about 5'9 somewhere between 160 and 200 lbs. Dark skinned with a fade with waves at the top. He was sexy, she wouldn't lie to herself.

"Look Latrease, I'm your doctor and I'm also your friend. Do you remember the last thing you did before you woke up today?" He asked hoping that she would cooperate.

"Sure I remember," she snapped. "I um…And then I…I can't remember! Is that because of the accident? Dr Harmon said I had been in one; did that cause me to lose my memory too? Is that why I don't recognize you?"

As the questions all came quickly, Randy wondered if indeed she did have AMD.

"I think you may be suffering a mild case of Amnesia."

"Well is there a cure, can you give me something to take to make it better I have to go to work?" she asked already knowing the obvious.

"There's no medical cure but I will prescribe you get some rest."

Latrease nodded her head then she remembered something that Dr Harmon had told her. "You said that you were my friend right?" Randy nodded.

"Do you know who my boyfriend is, and why wasn't he called?"

Randy hated to lie to her but he knew that it wasn't wise to tell her the truth, because it could make her forget him forever. He planned to work with her day in and out until she got her memory back, because they had a baby to raise and there was no way that he was going to raise another child from the outside looking in, point of view.

"I don't recall at this time, you ever mentioning anyone" he lied, but it was the only way to escape the question for now.

Latrease thought to herself for a moment. How I could be pregnant when I have no recollection of a man, she wondered. None what-so-ever! You would think that would be something that one would remember. "What do I do now, and when can I leave this place?" she asked with a fearful look on her face.

"I can't answer that, it's up to Dr Harmon." He then explained to her that he was not amongst the staff there at Hawervan. "We are in a different town, not in the city we live in. You don't have any relatives nearby that could come and get you. I highly doubt that they are going to let you go home in your condition. Not without someone to look after you." He told her not sure how she would take it.

It was eating him up that he could not take her home with him. He knew that she would NEVER agree to going anywhere with him, she only saw him as her doctor. He had waited for days for this day to come. The day she would wake up. It was nothing like what he'd dreamed. He'd had this day rehearsed in his mind, and now nothing was going as planned. In his dreams (*she would wake up asking for him, calling out his name. Doctor Harmon made a special call to get him there right away. He would walk in the room and she would be waiting for him wearing nothing but a satin gown and the heart decorated anklet that he gave her for Christmas. She would run to him arms open lips longing to kiss him. She'd be happy and on that day they would make love, really make love right there in the hospital room.*) He knew that it was just a dream and wouldn't happen, but at least in the dream she remembered him. At least in the dream, she remembered the feelings she had for him. He cursed himself as he felt the sudden erection poking at the crouch of his jeans. He wondered if Latrease had noticed. That was something that always happened when he was around her.

He was just about to excuse himself when she asked, "I don't mean to sound out of my league, but is it possible that you can take me home. I mean you *did* say that you were my friend right? Friends don't leave each other in sticky situations. Someone close to me told me that once although I can't remember who."

As much as he wanted to say yes, he had to tell her no. He couldn't see himself taking her home and leaving her there with no one to be there with her and make sure she was alright. At least with her being at the hospital he would be able to monitor her and she would be taken care of by the staff. He knew that he had to go back to Atlanta in two more days for sure because he had patients to see that had been rescheduled. He weighed out all options that came to mind then told her what he came up with.

"I can take you home, but on one condition, that is that you stay with me…"

"Excuse me!" she cut in, she knew that he said they were friends but what kind of friends were they? "Not exactly with me" he began to explain, "I have a guest house in the back of my estate you'll have your privacy and at the same time I can keep an eye on your progress."

After they went over a few more details she agreed to the arrangement.

The next day after Randy had packed up his things from the hotel room; he called his nephews and gave them instructions to clean up the guest house. He then stopped by the Valdosta Mall and bought an outfit for Latrease to wear home from the hospital. He realized that this was going to be the biggest test he'd ever taken. He knew that he couldn't make a single mistake or he could lose her forever. He would have to be extra careful.

At six o'clock that evening Latrease was dressed and almost ready to go. One of the nurses brought her a bag, which contained a purse, a black evening dress with a very enticing split. The nurse explained to her that these were the only items that were brought in with her the morning of the accident.

"You can check with Detective Wade at the police department to find out if anything else managed to survive the wreck."

The nurse handed her a card with the detectives' phone number on it and left the room. Latrease folded the dress along with the two satin gowns that Randy had previously brought for her. She then walked over to the mirror and looked at herself. She was wearing a pair of FUBU jeans with a pink blouse that matched. She wondered if her doctor was this generous with his other patients, if so he would have filed bankrupt by now. She grinned as she looked at the expensive clothes that she was wearing. Why this man was going out of his way to help her anyway, she wondered. She didn't understand. She had thought about this all night and still hadn't come to a conclusion. Maybe it was just the friendly thing to do, she thought, and was interrupted by a single knock on the door.

"Miss Wilson, are you ready to go?" asked Dr Harmon. Latrease looked at her and nodded. "Yes, sure." She replied, "I'm just trying to figure out what to do with all this hair." Dr Harmon giggled. "You have enough hair on your head for you, me, and about two of my nurses." They both laughed. "I'll see If I can find a comb and a barrette or something, be back in a minute."

A few minutes later Dr Harmon came back and handed her a comb and a huge rubber band. She helped her hold her hair in place while Latrease put the rubber band on it. "The second thing that I am going to do when I get home is to get this cut for sure." Latrease told the doctor while putting the comb in the bag.

"What's the first thing you're going to do?"

"Probably sleep for a couple more days" they both laughed.

***

Three hours later Randy and Latrease were turning into Honey Grove Circle. "There are four houses included in Honey Grove," Randy explained to Latrease. "My brother Bernard and his wife and kids live in the one on my left. My sister Shemeka lives on that side of him next to the entry way. My mother Ms. Bessie Scott lives next to me on the right hand side that puts me practically in the middle. There's a pool and tennis court on the left hand side of Shemekas' house."

Randy pointed out as Latrease looked with amazement. They were some of the most beautiful houses that she'd ever seen. They were well landscaped with lovely flowers and the bushes were all trimmed neatly at the same level. There were colored gravel along the walkway to each home and although they all looked very similar each home had uniqueness to it.

Randy checked his mailbox and then pulled into his remote controlled garage. As they parked Latrease noticed that there was a car already in the garage. She wondered if Randy was married or was there a live in significant other. Although she knew that this was none of her business she felt compelled to ask anyway, besides she was going to be practically living with these people. She needed to know.

"Is that your wife's car?" She asked, not sure if it had come out right. With a slight smile on his face, Randy answered, No, that's my car. I'm not married...why you ask?" a shiver went through her stomach. "I was just curious because I didn't see a ring on your finger." She shot back as she tried to figure out which car was more expensive, the Lexus that they had been riding in or the BMW that was parked beside it. She didn't know, but she did know that they both cost a lot of money.

After a twenty minute tour around the townhouse Randy decided to show Latrease the guest house where she would be living. "There are two bedrooms, a full bath is in the master bedroom and a half bath is in the hall, there's a full kitchen and if you need to do laundry you can use my laundry facility. Do you remember where it is?"

"I think I do, but I don't think I'll need it. I can wash my outfit on my hands." She replied. He realized that Latrease didn't have any clothes and offered to take her to the mall the next day.

"Here's the number to my house. After you shower we will go get something to eat." He told her as he placed the number on the table next to the phone.

"Thanks for the offer but actually I'm not hungry, a little tired though, I just want to take a long hot bath and then get some sleep. What time did you want to go shopping?"

"I'll call you in the morning, we can have breakfast at my place and then we will head to the mall." He answered and then turned to leave.

"Dr Jackson…" he interrupted, "you don't have to call me that. You can call me Randy. You always did."

"Well anyway, I just wanted to say thank you for being so generous and such a good friend. I don't know if I'll ever be able to repay you for this."

"You don't have to, just knowing that I was able to help is all the thanks that I need." He replied. "Randy, do you know about how long it's going to take…I mean I know that when some people lose their memory they never get them back. I wouldn't want to impose…"

"You are not imposing, besides your being here gives me a chance to study your condition at a more close up basis. You are not a burden; you are actually helping me as I help you, so to speak. So now, just relax, get some sleep and I'll see you in the morning.

After a long night of tossing and turning, Latrease woke up in the middle of the night to the sound of thunder. She suddenly became a victim of the rain as it pierced through the crack in the window that she had propped open before she went to bed. Latrease got up and closed the window. Instead of lying back down she decided to look through the purse to see if she could find anything that would help her figure out the many mysteries that had been running through her head ever since she woke up from that coma.

Inside the purse there was a smaller chained sized wallet. In the wallet she found her driver's license. There was also a picture of a little girl with a pink dress on and pretty long pigtails. The little girl was holding what looked like an Easter basket. There was a short stalky lady on the picture as well as a tall man. They were both dressed up too. There was no doubt in her mind that the little girl in the picture must have been

Latrease in the picture, perhaps eleven or twelve years old.

She took the picture out of the wallet to see if there was something written on the back of it, but when she took it out she saw something that was more interesting folded up inside the picture slot it was a folded up letter. She opened it and began to read...*Latrease, I know that it's been a couple weeks since we've seen each other, it is not your fault, its mine. When you told me that you loved me that night I didn't know how to react. I never meant for our relationship to become anymore than friendship. It's too risky. I didn't mean to leave the way that I did, that was childish of me. I didn't know how to tell you that I love you but I'm not in love with you. If in any way I lead you on to feeling that I wanted something deeper, I apologize I shouldn't have let things between us escalate this far. R.J.*

Who was R.J.? , she wondered. Could he be the father... she looked at the letter again, checking to see if she had missed anything. It was dated January 4th, 1999. It was now April, she wondered if it was possible. She then wondered how far along her pregnancy was. Dr. Harmon hadn't told her. She put the purse inside of one of the dresser drawers and went back to bed. She wasn't sure if it was because of the baby or just her own tiredness from the long ride that made her so exhausted. She knew that she had a long day ahead and she decided to finish looking through the purse later.

***

The next day Latrease rang Randys' door bell at ten o'clock am. She was wearing the outfit that she had worn the day before with the shoes that he had bought to go with it. "Good morning Latrease, I thought I was going to have to go shopping without you." He grinned and then asked, "How did you sleep?" Latrease smiled, "Other than the loud crashing of thunder, the faint sound of rain, and the hungry feeling that was at the pit of my stomach, I slept like a baby."

He laughed. "I knew you would be hungry last night, why didn't you call me I could have brought you something?"

"In the pouring rain! I wouldn't have wanted you to come all the way…"

"You're talking like you were far away or something. You must have forgotten that you're right in my backyard. Well anyway, you can make up for that this morning you can eat till you drop if you want."

"You can cook?" Latrease looked around with her nose in the air looking for a hint of what he had cooked. "I don't smell anything. What did you do, buy something already cooked?"

"Better! We're having breakfast at my mother's! I don't know how to cook toast, but I don't have to my mom cooks and I eat there."

"You mean, you and I are going to have breakfast with your mom? I'm not good at meeting other people's parents. I would feel so weird. I already feel awkward about being here and now you want me to have breakfast with your mom. Does she know about me, I mean the reason that I'm here?" Latrease asked him as she looked around the room.

Randy's house was big and pretty but she could see the loneliness in it. She could see that he didn't have anyone come in and decorate at all. The furniture was plain and dull. There weren't any pictures around the room either. She had wondered why the guest house was so well decorated, so homely, with matching furniture that must have cost a fortune, and his house so plain.

"Not exactly, I haven't had a chance to let them know about you yet." He explained that when he had tried to call from Valdosta they were all out.

"So are you ready?" he asked while admiring her.

"I guess I have no choice, I'm too hungry to protest."

Latrease and Randy walked next door to his mother's house. After about three knocks a woman appeared at the door. She was a little shorter than Latrease herself. She had long braids in her hair that reached the middle of her back. Her eyebrows were arched perfectly, and her makeup was just right. She looked like someone out of the movies kind of like *Angela Bassett*. This must be his sister; she thought but soon discovered it was his mother, when Randy introduced them, "Latrease this is my mother, Bessie." He then turned to the woman and said, "Mama this is Latrease."

"Good morning, it's nice to finally meet you. Randy's been telling me that he was going to bring you by but he never did. I was beginning to think that he made you up, especially since no one in the family had ever met you, and it's kind of hard to get around running into our family, but he's hid you good…"

"This is Latrease, my patient, not…"

"Don't try to change the subject Randy we all know what you're trying to do. Well anyway Latrease it's good to finally meet you. You and Randy can set the table while I go finish up in the kitchen."

After breakfast they went to Lenox Square Mall. They shopped for hours until she had everything she needed. Her total came out to almost five hundred dollars. Latrease felt weird letting him buy her expensive clothes, but he had insisted. She told him that she would have settled on going to the flea market, or even just going by her house to get some things, but he wasn't hearing it.

"Besides" he had said, "Everything I spend I can write off on my taxes so I prefer you to get things that you would want to wear when you go home too."

He had lied to her again. He hated it but it was the only way to convince her of why he was being so generous. He couldn't stand the distance that they had between them as they walked around the mall. They had passed so many couples walking together holding each other. It nagged him that he was walking beside such a beautiful girl and couldn't do anything to show how much he cares for her. He had even wished that he hadn't interrupted his mother earlier when she was talking to Latrease, but inside he knew he did the right thing.

Home! The word had ringed in her ears like a bell. Where was home, she wondered. What was she doing before she was in that horrible accident? Who was R.J. and was he the father of her unborn child? If so, where was he now? The questions kept coming up in her head. She couldn't understand she wondered if maybe Randy knew the answer to her questions. If he did he was being real good at not volunteering any information, for sure. Every time she'd ask about herself he'd sort of change the subject. It was as if he didn't want her to know her past. How else was she going to get better if she didn't know, she wondered. How was she going to figure out what she wanted to know if he wouldn't cooperate? What was his problem anyway? There were so many questions; Latrease decided that if she was going to find out all the answers, she was going to have to do the detective work herself.

Later that night after Latrease had finished putting up her new clothes she decided to take another look inside the purse. She opened the wallet and looked at the driver's license again. There was an Atlanta address on it. She figured that the address on the license would be a good place to start looking for answers.

How she could have not thought of this before, she asked herself as she looked in the bigger part of the purse. There was a trial size bottle of hand lotion, some deodorant, a brush, a couple of envelopes, and a picture album. She looked inside the picture album there was a Glamour Shot picture of her wearing a fur shawl around her neck. She had makeup on and her hair was pulled back in a bun. In that picture Latrease thought she looked like a model. There was another picture in the album with Glamour Shot marked on it. In this picture her hair was down and it was straight, dyed black. She was wearing a black gown with spaghetti straps and a thin jacket over it. The next two pictures in the album were similar but they had a different photographer's initial on them. On those pictures she was wearing swimsuits. These pictures must have cost a lot of money, she thought as she observed their professionalism. There were a few more pictures; they were all done efficiently, as if she needed them for something important. She didn't understand. Why would she need pictures like that?

***

DING! DONG! Latrease felt her heart jump to the startling sound of the doorbell. She put the album back into the purse and raced to open the door. She was shocked to see it wasn't Randy. Instead it was a woman.

"Hi, I'm Shemeka, Randy's sister. I hope I'm not interrupting anything. My step mom told me that you were here so I figured that I'd come back and introduce myself since my brother is being so rude. I don't know why he doesn't want anyone to meet you, you look twenty times better than anybody I've ever seen him with."

"Well actually he's not my boyfriend, he's my…"

"Oh my God!" Shemeka butted in, "My brother's getting married! I can't believe this! That would surely explain why you're living back here instead of up there in the house with him. Let me see the ring!" Shemeka asked and looked down at Latrease's hand.

"I'm sorry, but you have the wrong idea your brother is not my fiancé, he's my doctor!"

Shemeka giggled, "Sure he is, is that the best story that the two of you could come up with?"

Latrease didn't know what to say to convince her that she was telling the truth, but after a few more details about why she was really there, Shemeka gave up.

"I'm sorry; I guess I got a little carried away. It was more of the idea of him being settled down that caught my attention the most. Is there anything that I can do to help?" she asked.

"Umm, would you happen to know where Oak Street is?"

Shemeka thought for a minute, "Yea there's an Oak Street over in the West End, Is that the one that you are talking about?"

"I really don't know for sure. I've been looking through the remainder of my things and I saw an address on my driver's license on that street."

"What are you going to be doing tomorrow?" Shemeka asked looking down at her watch and noticing it was too late to attempt to go anywhere now.

"I don't have anything planned and Dr Jackson said that he would be returning to work in the morning. He didn't mention anything."

Shemeka laughed.

"What?" Latrease asked wondering why everything was so funny.

"I still can't get over my brother Randy trying to be Mister Nice Guy; it just hasn't registered in my head yet. Plus you said he took you to the mall and bought you all of this stuff this is truly not like my brother at all. Randy is the most stingy, cheapest guy that I've known my whole life and that's on the real." Shemeka knew her brother was up to something for sure.

"Well anyway how early do you get up?" Shemeka asked changing the subject but not forgetting what she had been thinking.

"Is eleven too early?" Latrease asked.

"No that's just fine, I'll see you then, and we can go find that address." Shemeka told her as she forced herself to hold back a smile. She knew Randy way too well to know that he was up to something. Latrease had appeared to be a nice girl and she deserved to know as much as possible about herself and her past. She wondered if that was really her brother's main intentions or if he had other plans as well.

On her way back home Shemeka thought about paying her big brother a little visit but then she figured that it would be a waste of time for she knew that one thing her brother was good for and that was keeping information on his patients confidential. Even though there was absolutely no way possible that Latrease could be his patient she decided to leave it alone for now. She knew that he wouldn't speak a word about Latrease's condition and that he would probably forbid her to help in any way. So she decided against confronting him.

The next morning at about a quarter till eight Latrease woke up to the sound of keys rattling at the front door. She grabbed her robe and ran down the hall to the living room. Not knowing what to expect, Latrease was relieved after she saw that it was Randy. She really wasn't sure how to feel, happy or mad.

"Excuse you, haven't you heard of knocking?"

"Good morning Latrease, I'm sorry that I woke you…"

"Don't good morning me, what are you doing here this early in the morning and why did you have to let yourself in? I thought you said I would have my privacy?"

Randy was flushed as he tried to explain. "I didn't knock because I didn't want to wake you…it's not what you are thinking, I was bringing you this."

He raised a bag that had been hidden behind his back ever since she'd come in. "I was on my way to the office and I remembered that there wasn't anything in the kitchen for you to eat. I stopped by IHOP and picked up some breakfast for you. On my way here I stopped by my mothers and she said that she would take you to the grocery store today when you got up. I didn't want to wake you up so I was going to leave a note on the table to let you know."

"Well thank you for the food, but I won't be able to go to the store with your mom today." Latrease walked closer to him. She hadn't realized that as she walked her loosely tied sash had started to come untied.

Randy tried not to look but he couldn't help himself. She was so attractive, even more now that she was off limits.

"Your umph thingy is open." He said while pointing to the sash. She retied the straps and grabbed the food.

"Do you mind telling me why you are not going to the store?" he asked wondering what could be more important being that she didn't know anyone around there.

"The last time I checked both or my parents were deceased. But since you must know I have something planned to do."

"Oh you do! Well I guess I'll see you later then, by the way here's a key to the house and a spare to my house in case you need anything that's not here." He handed her the keys and then left. Latrease stood there for a minute. Here heart was still beating fast from the sassy way she'd spoken with him. "You could have been nicer," she told herself but then remembered that he was the one out of line. He was the one that came in there trying to make orders. The nerve of him! She went into the kitchen and placed the food on top of the counter.

She had been hungry but he had spoiled her appetite. She went back to bed.

At ten o'clock Latrease woke to the beeping of her alarm clock. It was time for her to get ready. She went into the kitchen and put her breakfast in the microwave. She then went into the master bathroom and took a shower. She was sitting on her bed putting lotion on her legs when something caught her eye. "Why hadn't she noticed it before?" she wondered. It was an ankle bracelet around her ankle with her name in script. It was beautiful, shiny, gold with diamonds trimming around the letters. She undid the clasp and held it close so that she could see if there was an inscription inside. There was. It read "With all my heart, R.J." This was clearly a very expensive piece of jewelry. She examined it a little closer. It was gold and silver and every well cut. Whoever R.J. was he had good taste in jewelry, she thought to herself and smiled but the smile faded shortly after as she realized that she may never see R.J. again. She knew that she had to do her best and work hard and trying to remember her past so that she may be reunited with the love that she had been separated from. Could he be R.J.? She was almost certain now; it seemed all the signs were pointing to it. So now the hardest part would be finding him!

Later that morning, Latrease and Shemeka were riding up and down Oak Street. "I didn't know that there were so many parts to this one street. Latrease, do you recognize anything?" Shemeka asked her after they'd drove down that end of the street twice.

"I don't know, all these houses look alike. Could there be another end of Oak Street somewhere else?"

"I don't know, I saw a gas station at the next corner. I'll pull over and ask someone inside." Shemeka turned the car around and headed for the gas station. Inside she asked the clerk if there was a continuation of Oak Street on another block in the area. "Just go out the way you came in but instead of making a left go right and then go down about two blocks and there will be a fork in the road. Go left. There's an Oak Street about a block down on the right hand side. There are some apartments on that street. I forgot the name of them, though." Shemeka thanked the store clerk and then went back out to the car.

About five minutes later they were turning on Oak Street entering Oak Tree Gardens. Latrease's eyes widened as she observed the scenery. Latrease there's a security gate with a guard; I think that he will be able to help."

"Ok let's go over there and I'll show him my license and he can tell us if the address is within the complex. I have to admit Shemeka I do feel a little tingle in the pit of my stomach. I don't know if it's from being here or my nerves about it all." She didn't tell her that it could have been just the baby reacting to the brand new car smell of Shemeka's car. Shemeka had seemed like a nice person and she was very helpful but Latrease wasn't quite ready to tell her about the unborn child yet. Especially since she hadn't decided what she was going to do about this baby. She had thought about it over and over the past couple nights and she worried a lot about what she was going to do. It would be a whole lot easier; she thought if she could find out who the father of her unborn baby was.

They pulled up to the security window and spoke to the guard. "Hi my name is Latrease Wilson and I believe that I am a tenant here, well I think I am."

"What do you mean you think you are?" the young guard asked.

"I went out of town a little over a week ago and I was in an accident. As a result I have a bit of Amnesia." The officer looked sympathetic for her but then replied, "I'm sorry to hear about your accident but I don't think that I can help you ma'am."

"What do you mean, you can't help me…" he stopped her before she could finish, "How do I know you are telling the truth? Do you have anything that would prove that you lived here?"

Shemeka rolled her eyes. This man was being a total jerk. She knew that he was doing his job but he didn't have to act as if their being there was getting on his nerves.

"There's an address on my driver's license," Latrease explained as she handed him the license.

"I'm sorry if I gave you a bad impression, it's my second day here and you'd be surprised to see some of the stories that I've gotten." He explained.

"I understand." Shemeka said but was still a bit mad.

"Yes ma'am."The young officer mumbled under his breath as he looked on the list of tenants. You're in complex B-2. Would you happen to have your key?"

Latrease looked back inside the purse. She hadn't remembered seeing any keys in it but she double checked anyway. "No I don't think I have one." She looked at Shemeka.

"That shouldn't be a problem, I'm sure there's a manager's office and they should have a spare." Shemeka looked up at the young officer who was shaking his head.

"That's just it, the managers out of town, there is a maintenance guy but he is off today." Shemeka's anger grew bigger, "So basically there's no one around to help us. This is some real BS. As soon as the manager gets here he will be getting a call from my lawyer for sure."

"Ma'am, I know that this is a big inconvenience, and I'm sorry. I don't know what else to tell you." The officer apologized again but Shemeka was already turning the car around.

"Latrease is there anything else you need to do today before we head back for home?" Shemeka asked.

"Well Dr Jackson had said that your mom was going to take me to get some groceries, I probably should have gone, but I think it's too late to ask her now."

"That's fine I can take you and my brother can just pay me back."

***

The next two days seemed to drag on. Latrease did a lot of reading and cleaning. Randy hadn't stopped by at all. She didn't know if it was because of the way she had talked to him the last time she saw him or if he was just so busy with his other patients. She had sort of missed him. It had been so lonely those past days Latrease wished that somebody, anybody, would come back there and keep her company. She even found herself missing Randy more; she didn't know why she just did. She decided to look through her things again to see if there was something that she had missed. The card that the nurse had given her at the hosptital. How could she have forgotten about this, she wondered. She decided to give Detective Wade a call but then realized the number was long distance. Randy had given her permission to use the phone but he hadn't said anything about her making long distance calls. She decided to wait and ask him if it was alright first. Just to make sure.

A couple hours later, Latrease walked through the garden and through the gate to Randy's house. Just as she was about to ring the doorbell Randy opened the door. A smile was on his face as he invited her in.

"Hi there I was just thinking about you."

"Really! I can't tell! I haven't seen you in, I don't know how long!" she replied with a slight grin on her face.

"I thought that maybe you wanted a little more space, you weren't exactly happy the last time you saw me."

"It was early in the morning; I get a bit cranky in the morning especially when my sleep is interrupted." Latrease snapped back.

Randy realized that he hadn't invited Latrease in yet, they had been standing there talking through the screen door for about five minutes before he even noticed. He couldn't help himself but wonder what had been the reason for this unexpected little visit. Could she have remembered something? If so, what?

Latrease looked around the room and tried to focus her attention on anything but Randy. She couldn't help but notice that he was looking good. He was wearing a white muscle shirt with no sleeves, a pair of gray sweats, with gray and white Nike sneakers. His hair was looking good as well. Something about this man sent shivers up her spine. She didn't know if it was how fine he was looking, or the intoxicating fragrance he was wearing. She tried not to give him direct eye contact, or even let him sense that she was checking him out but she couldn't help herself. He was drop-dead-fine! She couldn't help but look.

"I didn't interrupt anything, did I?" she asked not sure how he took it.

"Oh no I was about to head down to the gym for a minute my brother had a couple of ideas and he wouldn't discuss them on the phone."

"You and your brother own a gym together? I didn't know that."

"Well actually my father left it to me when he passed. My brother was involved in some illegal things at the time when the will was being drawn up, so my father felt he wasn't responsible. Technically the gym was supposed to go to Bernard. After he decided to straighten up and that he wanted to be there for his family I gave him a job to run the gym."

Latrease smiled. "Well that was very nice of you."

"Hey if you're not doing anything, I mean if you don't have any plans would you like to come check the place out?"

Latrease grinned at his sarcasm.

"I don't have anything planned but I do need a few minutes to freshen up."

They decided to meet up in the garage in twenty minutes. Latrease went home and pulled her hair back into a ponytail. She put on a pair of gray shorts and a gray t-shirt with some low socks and a pair of white Reeboks sneakers Shemeka had given her a few days back. She wondered what Shemeka would say if she told her that her brother had asked her out, well not actually on a date but it was very close to one. Shemeka would flip, she thought. She still believed that there was some hidden agenda for having Latrease there in the first place. She decided that she wouldn't mention this to Shemeka, and besides they were just going to the gym and it wasn't like he was planning on inviting her.

"All set?" Randy asked as he watched Latrease enter the garage. "For a moment there I thought you were standing me up."

They both laughed. Randy opened the door for Latrease and she got in the car,

"Do you mind if I look at your CDs, Randy?"

"Oh no, sure they're in that case." He pointed.

"Oh my God! I can't believe you have this! I love this CD. Don't you just love his voice?"

Randy looked over at Latrease, he

couldn't see what the CD was. "Yeah hand it to me and I'll play it."

"Ok, my favorite song is track number 15."

Latrease handed the CD to him. He put it in the player and skipped to number 15. It was *R. Kelly's, If I Could Turn Back The Hands Of Time.*

Any other time Randy would have been singing along, but right then he wanted to cry. The song had really dampened his spirits for sure because he couldn't even bring himself to smile. All he could think about was how he felt when Latrease was lying in that hospital bed fighting for her life. As the song went on all he did was drive and tried not to look affected by the words. He kept having flashbacks of the way things once were. He missed the times that he and Latrease would be on their way out somewhere, and how they would be so distracted by each other's sex appeal that they wouldn't even make it to where they were going. They would go to the nearest hotel and spend the night loving caressing and holding each other.

He missed her so much and it wasn't just the sex that he missed either. It was more than that. Randy felt a tear roll down his cheek. The song was finally going off.

"Now that we heard your favorite R Kelly jam here's mine."

Latrease didn't know which song he was going to play, she liked that whole album. As the song began to play Latrease began to recognize it.

"*Half On A Baby*. This is my third favorite song."

They sat and listened to the song while Latrease looked at the other CDs in the case. A few minutes later they were pulling up at Big Brothers Gym.

"This is it? This place looks big enough to be a mall or something." She said.

"It is big but it's not *that* big. After I see what Bernard's up to I can take you on a little tour," he paused and then added, "if you'd like?" Latrease smiled, she could tell he was trying hard to stay on her good side and not sound pushy. "I would like that."

Inside they were greeted by a teenage

boy at the door. "What up dog?" The boy asked Randy and stuck his hand out to give him five.

"Kevin what have I told you about that? You never know who could walk through those doors."

"My bad it won't happen again, Uncle Randy."

They left the lobby area and turned into a room that appeared to be some sort of group room for meetings. Latrease studied the room for a minute and then looked back at Randy. There were two long tables that had been pulled together to make one, with about eight chairs up to them. There was a woman sitting at the table along with two men. They all looked at Randy as if waiting for him to say something. He didn't instead he pulled out a chair for Latrease. He then turned to the woman.

"Where's your husband, Bertha?" he asked.

"That's kind of rude, aren't you going to introduce your little friend to the rest of us?" Randy left the room.

"Girl, how could you have ever

hooked up with Mr. Arrogant here?" Before Latrease could respond Randy came back in the room with another guy.

"I'd like to introduce everyone to my guest. Everyone this is Latrease a close friend of mine."

He then turned to Latrease and said "Latrease this is my brother Bernard, you've already met his wife Bertha, I assume, well anyway this is Curtis and Fred, they are personal trainers here at the gym."

After the brief introduction Randy sat in the seat next to Latrease. "Ok Bernard you have the floor." Randy pointed out as his brother took at seat at the far end of the table.

"Everybody knows how business is real slow on Wednesdays and Thursdays, so I came up with an idea to keep the money rolling in. I was thinking that we could have a Karaoke Night." Randy cut in, "Of all the silly things you've come up with I must say this is the most ridiculous."

Latrease looked over at Randy. "I think it's a good idea, Randy."

"Yeah everybody don't think like

you…" Bertha blurted out.

"Ok Bernard, continue with your plans I seem to be out numbered here."Randy replied, shocked that Latrease would take Bernard's side. After a few more details Randy decided to give Bernard's idea a try.

"So about how long do you propose it will take to get everything situated?" Randy asked without giving Bernard any eye contact.

"Well if I hadn't already taken the initiative to draw up the required papers, and I've already gotten a license, it's really just a matter of getting a few signatures in place. After that we could have an opening show as soon as three or four months from now."

"Ok well does anyone else have any suggestions or ideas for Bernard?" Randy asked and then gave a hard stare in Latrease's direction.

He was standing now; Latrease wasn't sure if he was at all thrilled about his brother's plans. What if he was mad at here for making that outburst, she wondered. She was indeed out of place being that this place meant absolutely nothing to her. This was

Randy's business; she had no right butting in. Then again, she thought, maybe that was why he had asked her to come along. Maybe he needed her help to fend off that feisty wife of his brother's. Latrease looked up at him, he looked so good when he was mad, she thought, and then quickly reminded herself that she shouldn't be looking at him that way.

"I have a suggestion, if you all don't mind." Latrease said looking at everyone in the room but Randy.

"I mind!" Bertha's words were sharp, Latrease felt like they slapped her in the face.

"Bertha where are your manners? I'm sure that whatever Latrease has to say can only better the ideas we already have. Latrease I'm sorry, go ahead with your suggestion." Bernard snapped at his wife and gave her an ugly look.

"Well what I was going to say is that for the Grand Opening it would bring more people in if we have a contest with a nice prize." Bernard nodded his head in approval.

"What kind of prize were you thinking

of Latrease?" he asked.

"I'm not quite sure that depends of what you all can afford to offer." She answered feeling good that she was being included.

"Latrease, would you assist Bernard with getting prepared for this Grand Opening?" Randy asked.

"I would love to if it's alright with everyone." Latrease answered and then gave a quick glance in Berthas direction. Bertha was just sitting there rolling her eyes, but to Latrease's surprise she didn't object.

"Its fine by me, I can use someone with ideas as Latrease. She knows what the young people like."

"Anything else" Randy asked looking at the other two guys who had been quiet the whole time.

"Nothing here", Curtis said and then looked over at Fred who nodded his head that he didn't have anything to add.

"Well if there's nothing else I guess we are done here for today." Randy said as he stood up and leaned forward to help

Latrease with her chair.

"You still feel like going on that tour, Latrease?" Randy asked.

"Well actually I kind of want to hang around and talk to your brother for a few more minutes; if that is alright with you?" Latrease giggled at the thought that she must have sounded like a kid asking for permission to stay out past curfew.

***

After weeks of sketching and planning, Latrease and Bernard had finally come up with some solid plans for the Karaoke Night. She had spent almost every day at the gym working on ideas for the decorations, as well as how the seating was to be arranged. Bertha had even contributed a couple of ideas, although she still wasn't very fond of having this young attractive woman working so close with her husband, she was beginning to soften up with the sarcasm and unkind words that she was known for blurting out.

Latrease was becoming so involved in her work at the gym that she had almost forgotten about her current situation, and temporary living arrangements. She had been put on the payroll at the gym. She was making a salaried paycheck of two thousand dollars a month most of which she put into a savings account she'd opened up. She had tried to give Randy money for living expenses but he wouldn't have it.

She had hardly seen Randy, but didn't seem to care. She was finally apart of something. Her ideas were being used to create something big; something that she was interested in. She sat in the living room of the guest house one evening making up flyers to announce the Grand Opening of Karaoke Night at the gym; she was trying to decide between one that Randy's nephew Kevin had put together and one that Bertha had thought of. They both were good and eye catching but lacked something that she couldn't quite put her finger on.

A few minutes later, Latrease was startled by the sound of a knock at the door. Randy smiled at Latreasae, fiddled with the lock on the screen door that she had recently started locking.

"Just a minute!" Latrease said as she

managed to open the door.

"What's with the maximum security?" Randy teased as he closed the door behind himself.

"The better to keep uninvited guests away, my dear."

They both laughed.

"So what brings you to my neck of the back yard?" Latrease asked still grinning from the joke she'd made before.

"Well I was following a trail of gingerbread when I stumbled across this house made of cookies and peppermint."

They laughed again then Randy told her his true reason for the visit.

"I just wanted to check on you and see if you were alright. I also wanted to see if you were ready to make our first appointment since you have not been to my office since the accident."

Randy had stretched the truth with her again. He hated having to do this but he knew deep down inside this was the right thing to do. He knew that he would have to pretend that he really was Latrease's doctor even though he wasn't to prevent her getting suspicious of him.

It had been almost a month since the day he'd brought her home from the hospital and he knew that she would be curious if he hadn't started being a doctor to her. He had spent those weeks doing lots of studying and research on Latrease's condition.

He had talked to one of his colleagues that had treated a patient with AMD. Dr Richards was an excellent doctor that had focused his career on studying memory loss cases. He had even volunteered to speak with Latrease to diagnose the depth of her condition. Randy had told him that he would speak to Latrease and get back to him. He wasn't sure that he wanted Dr Richards discovering information about his relationship with Latrease, and that was exactly what he would find out. "No," Randy had thought to himself, he would have to do this on his own there was too much to risk. If it got out that he had been involved with one of his patients, even though she wasn't really his patient, but who would believe that.

***

Latrease shivered as cold water cascaded across her body from the steady stream of the shower head. The fruity aroma of soap made her feel good inside as well as hungry. It had been two weeks since her first session with Randy and she was feeling a little happy that they had finally started, despite the fact that she would have to tell him her innermost secrets, well not everything just the ones that she felt would help get her memory back. So far, though, Latrease had to admit that the sessions were going well. She was most impressed with the way that Randy composed himself during their meetings. It was as if he was a complete different person from the one she had been seeing at home and at the gym. He was very attentive, and professional. He was sympathetic as he listened to Latrease recall moments she had spent with her parents before they died. He even offered to drive her to Macon to visit their gravesites whenever she wished to go.

She couldn't believe the progress that they had made, even though she still hadn't been able to recall what was going on the night of the accident. She was certain that the pieces to the puzzle would be all back together very soon.

Latrease smiled as she looked at her reflection in the mirror, and then quickly her smile was replaced with a frown. With all the work that she had been doing down at the gym and her sessions with Randy she hadn't noticed that her stomach had started showing. She hadn't even started her prenatal clinic visits yet. She wondered if anyone had noticed it. Well if they did they never showed it. She figured she'd take extra precaution to make sure that no one discovered her little secret, not yet anyway. At least not until she figured out what she was going to do about it.

Latrease tied the sash on her robe, brush her hair back in a bow, and rushed out of the bathroom. She then pulled a chair up to the table in the living room that the phone was on. Latrease quickly scanned though the yellow pages in the phone book until she found what she was looking for. She then picked up the receiver and hesitated for a long moment. What was she going to say, she asked herself as she looked down on the page? She had never had to deal with an OB GYN before.

Latrease closed her eyes, and then dialed the number. She took a deep breath as she listened to the automated instructions that were on the recording.

"If you would like to hear instructions in English press one…" the lady on the recording said and Latrease pushed the button. " If you think you are pregnant and would like to come in for a free pregnancy test press one and stay on the line for further instructions…" Latrease pushed the button again and was put on hold. About two minutes later a woman answered the other end. "Nolan Family Planning Center, this is Adrian speaking, may I help you?"

Latrease took another deep breath and then spoke back into the receiver. "Hi my name is Latrease Wilson and I am calling to start prenatal visits." Latrease said uncertain if it was the right thing to say.

"Ok Miss Wilson have you already had a pregnancy test with a written doctors confirmation?"

Latrease then proceeded to tell the lady about the accident and that the doctor from the hospital in Valdosta had told her that she was pregnant. "Well, Miss Wilson I can try to get the information from the doctor in Valdosta but it could take up to a week to get the records. It would be easier for us to just give you another test and start from there. Whatever is more convenient for you?"

Latrease thought for a second and then replied, "Well if it would be easier I would rather come in and get a test done. Is there any way that you can setup an appointment with me over the phone?"
"Well actually we give pregnancy tests every week on Tuesdays and Thursdays between nine o'clock am and one o'clock pm. You don't have to make an appointment. We take walk-ins. Once your pregnancy is confirmed we will start your prenatal care."

Latrease looked down at her watch and realized that it was Tuesday. "What would I need to bring, and how much is the test?" Latrease asked and then waited for Adrian to reply.

"All you need is proper ID and a parent if you are under eighteen years old. There's no fee for the test, it's free. Do you have any more questions Miss Wilson?"

"Umm …no, but thank you for the information."

***

Latrease waited on the porch for Bertha. She'd been catching a ride to the gym almost every day for the last couple of weeks with Bertha. She'd grew quite fond of Bertha over the last few weeks. At first Latrease felt awkward around her. They would sit in the car the whole time in silence. But one day Bertha broke the ice and Latrease could finally relax with her.

"You know, when I first found out I was pregnant, I thought I was hiding it very well. Then one day my mom was in the kitchen getting some milk and cookies and she poured me a glass of milk and handed it to me. She said to me, Bertha you need to start drinking more milk because your body needs the calcium if you don't that bun in your oven is going to suck all the calcium from you." Bertha explained, "And then she went to bed. I was shocked!"

Latrease smiled. "How did she know you were pregnant?"

Bertha pulled the sun visor down to get the sun out of her face. "I don't know, she just knew. She said I had a glow, a motherly glow going on."

Latrease tucked her bangs behind her left ear.

"I guess it's the same way I can see that you are too. I sure hope Randy is going to do right this time"

Latrease looked over at Bertha and sighed "oh no Randy and I are not..."

Bertha put her finger up over her lips. "Shhhhh it's ok none of my business anyway, but if you ask me you are a hellova lot better than any of those chicks he use to go out with. At least you got some sense and plus you're smart."

Latrease smiled and thanked Bertha for the compliment.

"Between you and me I like you a whole lot better."Bertha whispered as they pulled up to the gym.

Latrease didn't want to ruin the bonding so she didn't correct Bertha on her assumptions. She knew that Randy had a four year old son. She had never met him but heard about him and his mother from Shemeka. She had told her the story of how Randy and Valerie had met and how they were not even in a relationship when Valerie ended up pregnant. She'd told Latrease that Valerie married another man a few days after Keyon was born. Latrease had been learning so much about this family she felt somehow connected to them.

As soon as they walked into the gym the strong stench of musky cologne, mixed with sweat and funk; caught Latrease's nose instantly. She ran to the restroom and made it there just in time to vomit in the toilet. She spent the next five minutes hurled over the porcelain bowl trying to get over this morning sickness. As weird as it was there was not a day that went by that Latrease forgot she was pregnant. She'd put so much into trying to hide it only to find that everyone already knew. Well if Bertha knew they definitely knew because Bertha was not the type to keep quiet.

Later that day, Latrease was awakened by the ringing of the phone that was sitting on the end table next to the couch she'd been taking a nap on.

"Hello..." she answered.

"Hi are you busy?" it was Randy.

"No was just laying here reading a magazine."

Earlier in the month Randy had brought her almost every new mom and parenting magazine he could find on the shelf.

"Would you care to join me for dinner I cooked a roast?"

"Sure what time?" Latrease glanced up at the clock on the mantel piece. It was seven fifteen pm.

"In about thirty minutes if that's ok with you." He answered.

"Ok I will be there at seven forty..."

"I will pick you up at seven forty." Randy interrupted.

"My, Randy you don't have to do that

it's just a few yards away…"

"I insist." Randy chuckled.

"Doctor Randy Jackson, are you asking me out on a dinner date?" Latrease joked.

"That's exactly what I am doing." Randy responded. "See you in a few!"

Latrease felt butterflies in her stomach, or was it the baby agreeing that she needed to eat. She hadn't had anything to eat since lunch and she was a bit hungry. She took a shower and started getting ready.

"Date!" she thought to herself, She wasn't sure how she felt about that. She knew Randy was very attractive but she never thought of him that way. Plus she'd heard so much from his sister and sister in law about his previous relationships she knew he wasn't the man for her.

If Latrease was going to fall for someone he'd have to be someone that was ready to settle down.

***

Randy walked through the garden

and onto the porch of the guesthouse. The air was thick and humid. It was warm. He was just about to knock when heard a sweet voice invite him in.

He opened the door and peeked his head in before walking into the living room.

"Just a moment!" He heard Latrease's voice coming from the bathroom. It had been three days since he'd seen her.

The last time they were together was on Thursday when he drove her to the clinic for her prenatal appointment. He'd been to every appointment thus far. He wanted to be there during this pregnancy. He didn't want to have to miss any of it, like he had with his son.

Latrease was five months pregnant. Randy figured that that must have been what she was going to tell him the night of the accident. On that doctor's visit the OB GYN had did an ultrasound. Randy and Latrease saw their unborn baby for the first time through the machine. They'd heard the heartbeat a couple times before but to actually see the baby inside her stomach was a wonderful thing for Randy. That night when he got home he cried a long overdue cry.

Randy had never cried over a woman before but that night all he did was cry. He thought about the way things were. How much he hated the way he'd treated Latrease before the accident. How he would deliberately tell her he was seeing other women so she wouldn't get too attached to him. How he'd wanted her to go out with other guys her own age. How he felt he could never love her or treat her the way she needed to be treated. How every time he made a pact with himself that he would leave her alone so she could just forget about him, he'd come back. How he'd been sending mixed signals and how now he'd ruined her life by getting her pregnant. How because of him she hadn't gone to Julliard. The best school there was for music, theater, and dance. All of which talents Latrease possessed. How she could be performing in plays and movies, but instead she was knocked up sleeping in his guest house.

"I hope you're hungry, I cooked a feast!"

"I'll be just a moment," she repeated.

"Ok take your time the food is not going anywhere." He giggled.

When Latrease walked into the living room Randy's eyes grew big as he admired her beauty. She was wearing a blue maternity dress that had a v-neck cut that made her boobs look so perky. The dress was short barely covering her thighs. She was wearing some white open toed sandals that had rhinestones decorated on them. Her hair was down and straight with a slight curl at the end. She was looking hot, very hot. Randy could not control the way his body was responding to seeing her this way. The past few months she'd never worn anything sexy.

She'd been wearing large shirts that were way too big, and maternity pants, or long dresses that almost reached her ankles. Randy had almost forgotten what her shape looked like. He hadn't even seen her legs in so long and now he was looking at them staring at him looking so nice and smooth.

Randy felt butterflies in his stomach. He was so turned on by her, and not just the way she looked either. Her smile, those pretty eyes, and the way she looked at him.

"You are so beautiful." Randy managed to get out.

"Thank you, sorry didn't mean to go overboard, you know I hardly get out so I thought I'd dress up a bit."

"No need to apologize, girl you look so good right now, I don't know if I want to take you out or sit you on a pedestal and just look at you."

Latrease grabbed her purse and walked over to Randy, pulling the door shut behind them, they walked through the garden to the house.

"It's a nice night out tonight." Latrease whispered barely loud enough to hear.

Oh but Randy heard her.

"Yeah it is, not too hot, not too cold, just right." He replied.

They reached the front of his house a few minutes later.

"You ever wonder what kind of song their singing?" Latrease asked.

"Who, what song, I don't hear nothing?"

"Be still," she whispered, "now listen,

and tell me you don't hear that beautiful singing?" Latrease closed her eyes.

"I don't hear nothing, but those crickets, and birds."

"Yes I wonder what kind of song their singing. If you listen closely you'll hear that they don't all sound alike. Each cricket is singing his own song. I think it's lovely."

Randy closed his eyes and listened as hard as he could to see if she was right about them making different sounds. Until then, he'd never paid attention to that.

"Yes they do sound different, I never noticed that before."

"I just wonder what kind of song."

Randy gazed at her lips while she stood there eyes closed. They seemed glow under the moonlight. Randy fought hard not to kiss her, touch her, and hold her. He longed to so bad.

"What do you mean what kind of song?"

"I wonder if their singing a happy song, or a sad song or a lonely song or even maybe a love song." Latrease answered.

"I don't know maybe I'll catch one and ask him."

Latrease smiled, "You're so silly."

"Well it's the only way to find out, or maybe I'll let you ask him since you love singing all the time too. Not that I'm complaining, I used to love hearing you sing." Before he could take it back, Randy realized he might have said too much.

"When did you ever hear me sing? What are you talking about Doctor Jackson?"

"Wow so I'm back to Doc now?" Randy snapped back. "You sang for me at the office a few times. You were auditioning for a play or something, and you wanted to know what I thought. "

"What play, I don't remember none of this, did I get the part? What happened?"

"Yeah you did, you were great! You have a beautiful singing voice. That's why you got accepted…"

Randy stopped himself, he almost slipped. He couldn't tell her this. Not now. It wasn't the time. She was pregnant. Pregnant with his child! He couldn't tell her now. It would only complicate things more. He couldn't let her go all the way to New York in the middle of her pregnancy. He couldn't tell her about that scholarship now. It just wasn't the right time. But when would be the right time? When would he be able to tell her how in the last few weeks he'd grown even fonder of her than before? When could he tell her that he was falling, falling…?

"Accepted? What are you talking about Randy?" Latrease stared at him with those confused brown eyes.

"Nothing, I don't know, I must have gotten you mixed up with another patient." Randy stepped forward and pushed the door open.

"Just forget about it" he said and waved his hand in a motion to invite her in.

"Forget about it?! Apparently I've already done that Randy; I don't want to forget about it! I want to remember! I want to remember who I am! My life! What I did! What my goals were! I don't want to be living in your guest house, and working at your gym forever! I have a child on the way. I have to be able to provide for my child. I have to be able to tell him or her who she or he is! Who his/her father is! I want to know things so I can remember, I need to know things! You seem to be the only one around here that knows anything about me, why won't you tell me Randy? Was my life that pathetic that you would rather not tell me?"

The questions were coming so hard and so fast Randy didn't know what to say. She was right! She did need to know the answers to those questions, and she was also right about the fact that he knew way more that he was telling her. Randy hated the situation he was in. There were only two options. He could tell her everything and risk her not believing him and never getting her memory back or he could wait and see if she will remember on her own. He knew what he had to do he just hated putting her through this.

"Latrease, honey, I am here for you, I will not let anything happen to you. You can stay here as long as you want!"

"That's just it Randy." Latrease placed her purse on the couch and sat down next to it.

"I don't want you to take care of me! What if you decide you want to go out on a date or something? I don't need you feeling like you have to worry about me and taking me to my appointments and everything. I feel like I am burdening you and your family enough. I need to be able to do this myself. I need to get myself together!"

Latrease started crying.

"I went to that apartment that I use to live in the other day. But nothing was there. The landlord said someone claiming to be my husband had some movers take everything. He has to be my boyfriend; he has to be worried about me. He has to be looking for me. Do you know him Randy, please tell me what you know?"

Randy swallowed a huge lump in his throat and tried to figure out what he was going to say. Latrease was so sad, she'd even started crying. This was no good. Not good for her, not good for the baby.

"Calm down sweetie. After you get some food in you we will talk about this more ok?" he assured her.

***

Latrease tossed and turned as she dreamed of a man. A black man. A black man lying next to her. A black man lying next to her in a strange bed. A black man lying next to her in a strange bed in a strange room she didn't recognize. A bed she didn't remember getting in. She could see him so clear. He was laying there next to her holding her. She could not see his face. Why couldn't she see his face? The faint sound of an infant whining in the background. A baby. Latrease reached her hand down under the covers her stomach was flat. She must have had the baby.

The strange man held her tighter, the baby calmed.

Who was this stranger? Where was she? Why did this room look a bit familiar? Whose bed was this?

Ringgggg! Ringgggg! Ringgggg! Latrease jumped up at the sound of a phone ringing. What a dream! She thought to herself as she grabbed the handle from the receiver. She hadn't even noticed that she wasn't in her own bed.

"Hey sweetie, did I wake you?"

Latrease pulled the hair that was trailing across her face, behind her ear.

"Yes, no I was just about to get up." She recognized Randy's voice.

"Did you sleep well? You were so tired last night you fell asleep while we were watching a movie. I carried you to the bed and I slept on the couch I hope you don't mind it was raining outside so I didn't want to take you out in that weather."

"No it's ok, good morning to you."

"My mom is cooking some breakfast for you she should be over in a minute to bring you a plate. I made a mistake this morning and grabbed your key so you're going to have to stay put till I get home."

"Oh ok that's fine then. I'll be here."

Latrease put the phone down on the receiver after talking to Randy a few minutes longer. She would be there most of the day which was fine since she didn't have any plans. She had the day off at the gym. She decided to give Shemeka a call just to see what she was doing.

After the second try she realized that Shemeka was probably at work too. She made the bed and then walked over to the dresser and looked in the mirror. She was wearing a long t-shirt that definitely did not belong to her. She decided to at least take a shower and put her dress back on.

She looked around the room trying to find the light switch and once she had she looked around the room some more. Randy's room was very big. It had really nice furniture and a very big canopy bed with a nice cherry wood finish. The comforter, skirting and drapes all were green with black trim. There were no pictures on the walls. The walls were bare tan colored. There was a cream colored lamp on the nightstand beside the bed and another on the other side. There was a huge rectangular shaped rug on the floor and a trunk with a pillow top at the foot of the bed. It was so clean in there it looked like a display room at a large furniture store.

A few minutes later Latrease was stepping down into the Jacuzzi style bath tub. It felt so good to relax and soak. She'd added some bubble bath she found in the linen closet to the water and made a mountain of bubbles. She lay there with her eyes closed and enjoyed the aroma of vanilla which was the scent of the candles that were all around the tub. She'd lit one of them and had the bedroom light off.

"Mmmm" she sighed as she stretched her legs out in the water. "I could definitely get used to this" The water was nice and hot. Not too hot but just right. She lay there daydreaming, soaking in the hot bath for what seemed like an hour but in reality was only about twenty minutes when she heard the doorbell ring.

Latrease grabbed the towel from the stand and tried to brush away as much of the bubbles as she could. She then patted herself dry and reached for the robe that was hanging on the handle in the bathroom. It was a bit bigger than her but with her belly being the size it was it made it a perfect fit.

"Coming, Mrs. Scott!"

She tied the sash and slid her feet into the slippers next to Randy's bed.

The door bell rang again. Latrease

opened the door to find a strange woman standing there with a little boy. She was tall, way taller than Latrease. She was very dark skinned. She had short hair and lots of jewelry on. She was pretty, pretty enough to be a model or actress.

"Hi…" Latrease stared at the woman on the other side of the screen door.

"Umm where is Randy, he is supposed to watch Keyon this week while I go out of town, Let me guess he hired you to sit with him?"

"No, I'm sorry, I'm just one of his patients."

"Excuse me? That was weak! What do you mean you're one of his patients? The last time I checked Randy was a Pediatric Psychiatrist, so unless he's having some kind of sessions with that baby in your stomach then what's really going on. Oh and the whole wet hair, bathrobe thing really gave you away, but…You know something it's none of my business! Randy is so fucked up like that, he would rather lie to everyone he know before being honest and just saying he has a woman! You know, you'll never get him to do that, he is afraid of commitment. Anyway, that's your problem not mine. Here are his clothes, medicine, a few toys and his favorite book. Tell Randy to call me I really need to talk to him, by the way I'm Valerie."

She opened the door and walked in the house placing a suitcase and huge duffle bag on the floor.

"I'm Latrease and Randy *is* my doctor. I was in an accident,"

"Hon you don't have to sell that to me. I have to go my plane leaves in 30 minutes."

She was out the door and in her car in less than a minute. Latrease was shocked! She couldn't believe this woman! Who did she think she was barging in like that and leaving this boy with a total stranger? What was her problem? And what about what she said? Why was she saying that Randy was a child psychiatrist?

Latrease knew that couldn't be true, or could it? What did she really know about Randy other than the detective said that his number was the last number she'd called the night of the accident from her cellular phone? What was she doing out driving that late at night in the first place? Why wasn't she home in bed? Why was she wearing that dress? Where was she going? Who else had she called that night? All these questions had been running through her head the last few months ever since she woke up from that coma. Why had Randy come to her rescue in the first place? Did he know more about her? Why hadn't he let them put her in an institution or medical facility that handled people in situations as hers? What was so different about her than any other patients? Why had Valerie said that Randy was a child doctor?

Latrease closed the front door and looked at the four year old who was now sitting on the couch playing with a toy truck. "Hi Keyon, I'm Latrease, I'm going to be watching you until your daddy gets home ok?"

Latrease smiled.

"I know, you my daddy girlfriend!" Keyon looked up from playing and then got on the floor on his knees and started pushing the truck across the floor.

"No I'm just your daddy's friend." she explained.

"Well how come I saw you and daddy kissing that time?" he responded and ran past her down the hallway.

"Kissing? I think you may have seen your daddy with another friend that wasn't me sweetie?"

Latrease decided she would finish dressing and then talk to the boy after first calling his dad.

"Keyon I want you to stay right here until I get finished dressing ok."

"Ok Miss Treasie."

Latrease hung the robe on the latch and slipped her dress over her head. So many things were going through her mind. She sat on the bed for a second. She needed to sort them out. She needed some time to think.

The phone rang.

"Hello"

"Latrease I am so sorry I totally forgot about Keyon. I am so glad you were there mama went to the hospital with one of the twins. He hurt his foot at school and the school called her since they couldn't get a hold of Bertha or Bernard. I can be there in thirty minutes I just have to have Stacy cancel all the rest of my appointments for today…"

"You don't have to do that Randy I can watch him. I do have some things I need to discuss with you. I will wait until I see you in person, by the way what happened to our little talk we were supposed to have last night?" she remembered.

"You fell asleep, sweetie. I have to go my ten o'clock just showed up, I will call and check on you at lunch time there's leftovers in the fridge. Plus I just bought groceries yesterday so there should be plenty for you and him to snack on as well. Thanks a million Latrease I owe you one."

Oh he definitely owed her alright. Latrease put the phone on the hook and walked over to the dresser. She grabbed a brush and started brushing her curls to the back.

Then she went back in the living room

with Keyon. He had fallen asleep on the couch.

Latrease was hungry so she decided to fix something to eat for her and Keyon. She pulled out some eggs and bacon from the refrigerator and started cooking. She made toast and oatmeal as well. It was easy getting around Randy's kitchen. Nothing was hard to find, it almost felt like she'd cooked in there before.

***

The day went by fast for Randy. He'd wanted to call and check on Latrease and his son but he didn't want to run into any more questions from her that he couldn't answer. What a task it was to try to not tell her things about her past in order to keep her from forgetting them permanently. He had done more study of her condition. The more he learned the more he knew it would be a big challenge. He wondered how much longer he could do this. It had been so hard and even though he'd managed to keep her suspicions down from him, last night was even harder. Last night was the hardest. Why had he asked her over for dinner? That had turned out to be a big mistake. He felt horrible about giving her those sleeping pills in her drink. But he had to! He had to buy some time. He had to get her to fall asleep so he could avoid the subject. But how was he going to keep avoiding the subject. How was he going to keep her from asking? How was he going to keep her from wanting to know about her past? How was he going to stop her from digging and searching for answers? So far all his efforts had been successful but what was going to happen if there was something he'd overlooked and she found out about?

Keyon! Randy thought about his four year old who had been around Latrease a lot before the accident. Keyon was alone with Latrease! He'd definitely remember her. He'd definitely remember them hanging out together. It was only a matter of time before he would get that call from Latrease yelling at him and wanting to know what was really going on. Randy decided he needed to leave work. He needed to get to the house as soon as possible. He told Stacy he needed to leave, grabbed his briefcase and was out of the office in less than five minutes.

Randy turned onto Honey Grove Circle a few minutes past two pm. He was surprised to see that his mom's car was still gone. Bertha and Bernard was gone too. Shemeka was at work he knew that. He pushed the button on the car garage and pulled in then parked.

Randy put his key in the keyhole and opened the front door. The first thing he noticed was the TV which was on Barney. Keyon was on the floor playing with a toy truck when he looked up and saw Randy. He ran and jumped in Randy's arms.

"Daddy!!!!" the boy screamed in excitement.

"Hey Big Boy, Daddy came home early just to see you!" he told him while giving him a hug.

"Daddy did you bring me any presents?" Keyon noticed that Randy was holding something behind his back.

"Yes I did."

He told him.

"Did you bring something for Miss Treasie too daddy?"

Randy looked over at Latrease who was sitting on the couch smiling.

"Yes as a matter of fact I did bring something for her too."

"What you bring, what you bring daddy?" Keyon jumped up and down.

"Just a minute little booger let me talk to Miss Latrease for a second."

Randy placed the huge brown paper bag on the counter in the kitchen then walked over and sat down in the recliner chair that was facing the couch Latrease was sitting on.

"Thank you so much for watching him for me. Did he give you any problems?"

"No he was very sweet, full of energy." She replied.

"Yeah that's Keyon, vibrant and full of energy."

"Well he's a really good boy, well mannered for four years old and so very smart too. He knows his alphabet; he can count to one hundred. He knows most of his colors, shapes, and can read some words too."

"Wow I didn't know he knew all that."

"I really enjoyed him. I need to get home and have a shower, do you have my key?" she asked.

"You can't go yet I haven't given you your gift. As a matter of fact I wanted to take you and Keyon out to dinner, would you like to go, we can go where ever you want?"

"I'm sorry Randy I don't feel so good I'm just going to go have a bath and take a good long nap. I will come watch Keyon tomorrow if you need me to though."

Latrease gave the boy a hug, grabbed the key and was on her way over to the door when Keyon started crying.

"What's the matter sweetie?" She asked heading back over to the couch. Keyon rubbed his eyes. "I don't want you to go."

"Awe sweetie I will be back tomorrow," she replied.

"But I want you to come eat with us. And watch TV and bake cookies like you use to."

Latrease looked at Randy.

"What is he talking about Randy?" she asked

"Keyon you are mistaken." Randy tried to convince the four year old that it was not Latrease that he'd seen before.

"No daddy I want Miss Treasie to stay. I want her to sing for me, she always sing pretty song for me. Don't you Miss Treasie, don't you sing pretty songs for me?"

"Keyon I never sang for you. I don't even think I can sing." Latrease grabbed a paper towel off the counter and wiped the tears from his face. "But I will come back after I have a shower and we can go eat wherever you want to go. Ok?"

Randy stood up and pulled Latrease to the side. "What's going on, Randy? Why does he think he knows me?" Latrease asked.

"I'm going to have a talk with him go ahead and have your shower what time do you think you can be ready, I'm just going to throw on some jeans we can take him to

Show Biz Pizza he would like that"

Randy told her.

"I can be ready in about an hour." She replied and then left the house.

***

Latrease stepped out of the shower and grabbed the towel from the rack. She wrapped it around her body and dried herself while looking in the full mirror that was on the back of the bathroom door. Her belly was getting bigger. She'd gained 6 pounds since she left the hospital a few months back. She could now clearly see her belly and the dark black line that had started from her belly button that went down to her pubic area. She could feel the baby move and kick a lot too. Sometimes it was sudden and sometimes she knew the baby was in there playing and flipping and rolling around.

Latrease put on a bra, a white t-shirt, blue jeans and some white Fila sneakers. She wanted to be comfortable at the Show Biz Pizza place. She sprayed a dash of perfume on her neck and rubbed some on her wrists. She then put on a pair of cubic zirconium earrings, grabbed her purse and was out the door. The afternoon breeze was nice. It wasn't too hot or too cold. It was just right.

Latrease thought about all the things that had happened that day. The woman, Valerie who insisted she'd been lying about being Randy's patient. The child, Keyon, who swore he knew her and even called her Miss Treasie without her having told him her name. Who'd told her she sang to him. Randy had even said that the night before that she liked singing.

Then she started to think more about Randy. What was really going on with this man? Why did he act so peculiar all the time? Why was it that whenever she went to his office for a session there was never any other patients around? Why had his family opened up and accepted her so easily? Why had he been so interested in her pregnancy that he went to every doctor's appointment? Something was definitely amiss with this guy, but what was it? What was he hiding? Maybe it was all a coincidence. Maybe she was just reading too much into it. Maybe she wanted so badly to get her memory back that she was beginning to imagine things, imagine conversations, had the woman really said those things to her or had she imagined the whole thing? Had the child really said he'd seen her or was he just imagining too.

Latrease thought about it all, over and over. How could she have imagined those things? It wasn't possible! There was something, something Randy was not telling her. Maybe he knew her parents. Maybe he was her doctor when they died. No, that didn't make sense either but it would explain why he was so concerned and took good care of her now.

Latrease knocked on the door and was greeted by a flash of a camera.

"Miss Treasie look what I got!" the boy held his hand out and showed her a digital camera.

"I want to get a picture of you and daddy now." He was full of energy as he grabbed her hand and led her to the kitchen where Randy was.

"Hi" she mustered.

"Hello beautiful."

"Yall wearing the same clothes" Keyon noticed that Latrease and Randy were both wearing a white t-shirt and blue jeans.

"Stand together so I can take your picture." Keyon motioned for Latrease to get closer to Randy.

"Say cheese." He said and snapped the picture. Randy grabbed the camera and started laughing.

"Well Keyon we know photography won't be your profession heehee" Randy giggled while showing the picture to the boy. "But you did take a perfect picture of your thumb."

"Awe dad let me try again, this time I want yall to laugh a little for the camera."

Randy stood behind Latrease and put his arms around her, Latrease was holding her belly a little not really trying to hide it but just holding it. Randy tickled her a bit and Keyon snapped the picture.

"Perfect!" The boy ran over and gave the camera to his dad.

"You guys look great together."
Keyon said and smiled and hugged Latrease.

"Ok let me get a few of you and your dad. Keyon go stand over there with Randy." Latrease grabbed the camera and took a picture of the two of them.

"So who's ready for some fun and pizza?" Randy asked and grabbed his keys.

"MEEEEEEEEE!!!" Keyon jumped and yelled.

"Ok let's go." Randy replied.

A few minutes later they were pulling out of the garage. Randy had fastened Keyon into his booster seat.

Latrease enjoyed the scenery on the way to the restaurant. Keyon could just about name every type of car they passed. He knew them by name. When they got to Show Biz Pizza there weren't many cars there.

Keyon had already unfastened his seatbelt when Randy opened the back door.

"That's a no no Keyon, I don't want you doing that ok."

"Ok daddy can I bring my camera in?"

the boy was still holding it.

Latrease grabbed the camera. "I'll hold it for you sweetie."

About four hours later they were finally pulling up in Randy's driveway. Keyon was asleep. Latrease had nodded off too. "We're home!" Randy opened the car door and unbuckled the seatbelt for the boy.

Latrease picked up her purse and opened the door grabbing the camera that had fallen on the seat.

"I had a good time Randy." She smiled.

Randy was carrying the boy up the steps when he turned around and asked if Latrease would get the door. She grabbed the keys and opened the door. Randy carried the boy to the couch and laid him down.

"Randy we need to talk" Latrease sat down on the love seat.

"I know sweetie, I know."

"Randy when Valerie was here earlier, she said some things that…"

"Valerie does not know what she is talking about you can't listen to anything she says."

"Randy don't cut me off, you didn't let me finish." She was trying not to be too loud but the boy woke up.

"Even your son seems to think he knows me." She looked over at the boy who was wiping his eyes with his hand and yawning.

"Latrease he was mistaken. He's only four years old. He thought you were someone else." Randy explained.

"Someone else named Treasie?" Latrease rolled her eyes a bit. "I don't think that's possible."

The boy sat up. "Ask him now he will tell you."

"Keyon have you ever seen me before today?" She looked at the boy who held his head down and replied. "No, no ma'am."

Latrease was shocked. "Are you sure Keyon?"

The boy jumped in his dads lap and hugged him. "No never saw you."

"See Latrease, I told you he probably just thought you were someone else, that's all. Now I'll walk you home, my sister is going to watch him for me tomorrow. I know you have things to do at the gym with the karaoke night project just around the corner and all."

Latrease stood up, slung her purse on her shoulder, leaned down to hug and kiss Keyon goodnight. "Yea I do." She replied.

"I had a great time with you Keyon. Good night sweetie." He hugged her and then laid back down on the coach.

"Randy you don't have to walk with me I want to hang out in the garden for a while. Clear my mind a bit. Ok?"

She was out the door before he could say anything but "good night".

That night she couldn't sleep. She couldn't stop thinking about everything that happened that day. How Keyon had said he knew her and now was saying he didn't. She cried. She cried for a long time. She couldn't help herself the tears were falling so fast. Her stomach hurt. Part of her wished Randy had never come and got her from that hospital.

She hated being alone. She hated not

having any friends, any family she could call on. She had Bertha and Shemeka but they were Randys family, not hers. She needed to be around people that she knew; people that cared about her. She felt like she was at the end of a dead end street. No way through, nowhere to turn, no way to go except back.

Latrease got up out of bed and turned the television on. She found a channel that was showing music videos. A song was on. One she knew. She started singing along. She sounded good. No she sounded damn good. She realized something about herself. She did have a magnificent singing voice. The song went off and another came on. It was, *You Remind Me by Mary J Blige*. She started singing along with it.

Singing this song felt good. Latrease stood up and started dancing a bit too. When she did go to sleep that song was still in her head.

***

After giving him a bath Randy tucked his son in the queen size bed in the guest room. He felt awful having made his son lie to Latrease. He remembered the conversation he had with him earlier that day when Latrease had left to get ready for Show Biz Pizza. He had told Keyon that he needed him to pretend that he really didn't know Latrease. He'd told him to pretend this was his first time seeing her and that she had never ever sang for him , or went on any picnics, or to the fair , or zoo or any of the things they'd did before. He needed Keyon to pretend none of that ever happened and if he could do that then there would be a big surprise.

Randy hated every bit of it but he knew it had to be done this way.

***

The next weeks went by rather fast for Latrease. She tried not to spend time around Randy and his son. She'd go to work every day even on the weekend. She was now in her third trimester so she only had to see her doctor once every two weeks. Every once in a while Randy would stop by but she would push him away by telling him she was napping or just plain busy. She had decided she would take advantage of this opportunity to save money for her baby and that was her focus, getting on her feet. She didn't have time to waste spending with Randy. She had come to terms that he was not going to tell her anything valuable about her past and she had gotten to a point to where she really didn't want to know anymore. Her focus now was on her future and her unborn child's future. Not her past.

"Ok so we have two weeks before the Grand Opening of Karaoke Night." Bernard drew a circle around the date on the calendar that was hanging up in the meeting room.

"Talent Night" Latrease corrected him.

"Yes that's what I meant." Bernard shrugged his shoulders.

"I'm thinking about singing a song, as the opening not part of the competition of course." Latrease said.

"Ok sounds good to me."

Bertha then asked. "Ok so we have two weeks to get this on every black radio station, in the paper, and all over the TV right?"

"Yes!" Bernard responded and pulled

up a chair. He handed them all a folder with some flyers and press release forms inside.

"Ok well it's going to be a lot of work, but it will pay off. Especially since the car dealership donated a brand new car as first prize in exchange for advertisement and promotion."

"Yeah everybody and they granny going to be in here trying to win that car." Bernard agreed.

Latrease and Bertha spent the rest of the afternoon making rounds to the local radio stations. They dropped off flyers around town and put a full page ad in the local paper as well as all of the low budget papers too.

It was after seven pm when they turned into Honey Grove Circle. Randy's mother had invited the whole family for dinner she had fried a turkey. At first Latrease was not planning on going, she was planning to just heat up a frozen pizza in the oven for dinner but after the long day she'd had at the gym and all over town she decided she would go.

It took less than thirty minutes for her

to take her shower and pull her hair back into a ponytail and she was on her way up through the garden and past Randy's house to his mother's house. She was so tired she didn't even notice the eight foot stork in the yard. When she rang the door bell she was greeted by Shemeka.

"Come on in Latrease" Shemeka gestured for Latrease to come in.

"Surprise!"

Latrease looked around the room. There were so many gifts all over the place. She didn't know how to respond.

"Oh my God is this for me?" she asked giving Shemeka a hug.

"You're the only one in the room about to have a precious bundle of joy aren't you?" Randy's mother walked over and hugged Latrease as well.

Latrease was shocked. Her cheeks were red with excitement. There were so many packages all over the room. Bertha and the twins were there smiling.

"Come on in and have a seat Latrease we decorated this chair just for you." One of the twins said while pointing at the chair that had ribbons on it and a big bow. Latrease walked over and sat in the chair. She couldn't stop smiling as she looked around the room. There were diaper pins and bow confetti all over the floor. There was a section of the room that had nothing but stacks of pampers. There were so many baby gifts Latrease wanted to cry. Why were these people so nice to her and doing so much for her? She didn't understand.

"Thank you all so much I don't know how I'll ever repay you for this."

"Repay us? Girl you don't have to repay us. This is the least we could do. We know that baby will be here any day and we want her or him to have everything they need." Shemeka told her and walked over and gave Latrease a hug.

"I am speechless!"

One of the twins turned the stereo on and started playing some music. There were only a few people there, Randy's mom, Shemeka, Bertha, the twins, Randy's secretary from the office, all of which Latrease already knew, but there were enough gifts to get this baby through a whole two years.

Randy's mom had cooked a great meal. She fried a turkey, made macaroni and cheese, green bean casserole, stuffing, sweet potatoes, and lemon cake with chocolate frosting.

After eating there were a few baby games and then Latrease started opening the gifts. There were all sorts of baby clothes, blankets, pacifiers, bottles, toys, a crib, a bassinet, a high chair, a tub, a potty, crib mobile, skirting for the crib, a changing table, just about everything one would need and even things Latrease hadn't even thought of was there including a grooming kit , thermometer, and a towel with hoodie made into it.

Randy showed up just as the guests were leaving. He, Bernard and the twins started carrying the gifts to Latrease's house. She told them to put them in the extra bedroom.

Randy was looking extra cute that night. He was wearing some kakhi slacks and a blue dress shirt. He smelled so good when he hugged her she didn't want to let him go. But she had to. When she pulled her arms away her bracelet got stuck in one of his cufflinks it made it pop off. She reached down and picked it up and saw something that caught her attention and she couldn't quite figure out why. The cufflink had the initials R.J. on it. She wasn't sure why her stomach rumbled when she saw that or where she had seen it before but there was something about that moment; the way Randy smelled, the way he smiled something about that moment that made her feel jibbery.

Latrease thanked everyone and went to bed. She was tired and this had definitely been a busy day for her. She turned the TV on while lying in bed and watched the music video channel. As she fell asleep the lyrics to the Mary J Blige song was in her head again.

Latrease tossed and turned then finally was in slumberland.

Latrease tossed and turned as she dreamed of a man. A black man. A black man lying next to her. A black man lying next to her in a strange bed. A black man lying next to her in a strange bed in a strange room she didn't recognize. A bed she didn't remember getting in. She could see him so clear. He was laying there next to her holding her. She could not see his face. Why couldn't she see his face? This time she saw something else. She saw his chain around his neck. A gold chain with big letters. What did they say? She couldn't make it out. The faint sound of an infant whining in the background. A baby. Latrease reached her hand down under the covers her stomach was flat. She must have had the baby.

The strange man held her tighter, the baby calmed.

Who was this stranger? Why was he invading her dream yet again? Those initials...what was it about those initials?

***

Three weeks later Latrease was thirty seven weeks pregnant and still hadn't learned anything about her past. Even though she tried not to think about it the closer she got to her due date the more depressed she got about bringing a baby into the world with no family to help her, and not knowing who the father was. She hated that empty feeling. She had told her OB GYN she didn't want to be told what she was having. She remembered promising her mom that if she ever had a baby she would not find out until the baby was born and that was a promise she was keeping.

She'd been saving as much as she could from her job at the gym. She didn't want to wear out her welcome.

The Karaoke night was a blast. She had so much fun being a part of it. She had song *Whitney Houston's Run To You* and received a standing ovation. Everyone in the place stood up and clapped and whistled. After the show people were coming up to her asking for her autograph. She felt like a star.

There were three semi finalists who would be singing this night to move on to the finals. Latrease was asked to sing again to open the show. She wasn't nervous at all however her stomach had been cramping a bit earlier. She put her makeup on and brushed her hair down and straightened it with a flat iron. She'd picked out a beautiful blue and white dress to wear that accented her shape despite her huge belly.

She was ready to go when Randy knocked on her door. When she opened the door she was surprised to see Keyon standing beside his dad. The boy gave her a big hug.

"Daddy said I can come and hear you sing tonight Miss Treasie , I can't wait! Do you know what today is?"

Latrease looked at Randy and then down at the boy.

"No what's today?" she asked.

"My birthday I'm five years old!" he shouted.

"Oh my well happy birthday to you~~~" she sang.

"You sing so pretty Miss Treasie! Just like you used too!" Keyon hugged her again. Then put his finger over his lips. "Oops!" he whispered and looked at Randy.

Randy looked at his son. He had just finished talking to him before they walked up to Latreases door and yet it was as if all of it went out his other ear. Randy didn't need anything to happen that would cause any problems for Latrease now especially with her being so close to her due date. He didn't need her having any complications. It was hard enough since the last few weeks she had went to her appointments without him. He didn't like it but he didn't want to force himself on her either.

"You look gorgeous!" he told her while grabbing her coat.

"I hate that I had to miss last week's show I heard you blew the house out!" Randy smiled. He felt bad about missing the show but he had some business to take care of that couldn't wait.

Latrease was looking awesome. Randy wanted to hold her, kiss her caress her, all the things he use to do with her that he couldn't do now. He hated having to restrain himself. He hated having to sleep alone. The last few weeks she wouldn't even have dinner with him anymore. He hated it. He missed her so much but didn't know how to show it. When she had agreed to let him give her a ride to the show that night he almost jumped for joy.

"It's probably a good thing you weren't there I might have been nervous about singing in front of you." She smiled.

Less than a half hour later they were at the gym. There were many cars there and the lines were quite long but Randy decided to park in the owner's area and go in through the back way.

"I'll take his bag into the break room Randy and meet you guys in back stage." Latrease said and grabbed Keyons bag from the car.

"Does anything need to go in the fridge?"

"Yeah there are some snacks in there." Randy replied.

"Ok." Latrease disappeared in the building.

Randy unbuckled Keyon from the booster seat and carried him out of the car. They went into the building where he looked for Bernard.

Latrease grabbed the container of applesauce out of the bag and placed it on the shelf in the refrigerator. She then reached in the bag to get the sandwich and something fell on the floor. She reached down to pick it up It was a picture, a Polaroid of her, Randy and Keyon sitting on a blanket at what looked like a picnic. Her hair was shorter and full of curls and she was not pregnant. She knew it was her in the picture. Her mind began to race a million miles an hour. She couldn't breathe. Her head started spinning and before she knew it she was out cold.

She saw the man again. The black man. The black man lying next to her. The black man lying next to her in the strange bed. The black man lying next to her in the strange bed in the strange room she didn't recognize. The bed she didn't remember getting in. She could see him so clear. He was laying there next to her holding her. She held him back. She ran her fingers down his chest. Placed her lips over his. Pressed gently. Mmmm he tasted good. He smelled good. His lips were heavenly and she loved every bit. She closed her eyes she didn't want this moment to end. She didn't care what his face looked like. She didn't care what his initials were. She just wanted to be there with him, holding him, kissing him, feeling him between her thighs. He felt good. He smelled good. He tasted good on her tongue. She heard the faint sound of an infant whining in the background.

Noooooooo

***

Randy and Keyon sat in the front row eager and waiting for Latrease to come out and sing her song. Bernard came out and started going over the rules and announcing the semifinalists that would be competing. He then introduced Latrease who didn't come out on the stage. He looked around the room there was no sign of her. One of the twins that were sitting next to Bertha got up and started looking through the crowds. Randy stood up and looked around.

Bertha ran in the show room. "Randy she's unconscious and her water has broke!" she yelled and ran back into the break room. Randy ran behind her down the hallway and into the break room.

The emergency responders were there in less than ten minutes. Latrease had her eyes open and she was aware that she was going in labor. Randy wanted to ride in the ambulance with her but the paramedics told him to just follow in his car. Bertha stayed and cleaned up the floor and Bernard finished with the show. One of the twins rode with Randy and Keyon.

"Unk is she about to have the baby?" The boy asked.

"Yes I think she is." Randy replied.

"Then, what? Is she going to move out or will she stay in the guest house. Are you going to call any of her family to come to the hospital?"

Randy was trailing behind the ambulance trying to stay focused. The questions were coming hard and fast. "She doesn't have any family here."

He circled the hospital parking lot a few times trying to find a close enough spot.

"Daddy, if Miss Treasie has her baby today then it will have the same birthday as me." Keyon told his father while stepping out of the car.

"Yes you are right Keyon."

They hurried into the building and to the waiting area in the maternity ward.

Randy went up to the nurses' station and began talking to one of the nurses.

"Ok and who are you to the patient sir?" She asked.

"I'm the baby's father." Randy had never said those words out loud since he found out Latrease was pregnant but he felt it was time, time to tell someone even if it was this nurse he didn't know, that didn't know anything about them.

"Ok Dr. Jackson she can have two people in the delivery room with her but the child can't go in." The nurse told him.

"I know."

Randy walked over and grabbed the courtesy phone that was in the waiting room. He dialed Valerie's number then after the first ring decided to hang up. He was going to ask her to come and pick up the boy but changed his mind. Keyon was about to have a baby sister or brother even if he didn't know it. Randy wanted him to be there. Randy walked over and told his nephew to watch Keyon and that he would be back out soon.

***

Twenty hours later Latrease was exhausted. She'd given birth to a six pound three ounce baby girl. She was precious with curly dark brown hair. Latrease had her at eleven fifty eight pm.

She'd blanked out twice during the delivery and both times she dreamed. She dreamed of her parents. How she'd missed them. How she'd wished they never tried to make it that night. How she'd wished she never invited them to her play. How she'd wished they would have just waited to watch it on the VCR player. How she'd been in the middle of singing when the director stood offstage with that sad look in his eyes. How she'd cried so hard. How she thought she would never be able to move on. How she'd wanted to die when she saw their bodies at the funeral home. How she'd called all the family she had and none showed up. How she'd disowned the rest of her family. How she'd drove in her car with the music blasting. How she'd been so tired. How she'd ran off the road. How she'd sat in her car on the side of the road in the middle of nowhere for hours. How she'd seen headlights from the road. How she'd met a stranger and went home with him the same night. How she'd ended up falling in love with that stranger. How she'd taken the remainder of the life insurance money and moved to the city. How she'd gotten pregnant by that man!

Randy had been by her side throughout the whole delivery. She couldn't understand why he had lied to her. All these months lie after lie. What was so hard about telling the truth? Was it that he didn't want a relationship that bad that he was willing to try to make her forget everything? Was that why all these month he never really told her anything about her past? Was that why he would rather tell his family that she was his patient than tell them the truth? How could he be so selfish! How could he?

Latrease thought very hard about this while Randy was down at the hospital cafeteria with his nephew and son. She couldn't believe how he'd stooped so low to even have that sweet little boy lie. She thought about all the things that he'd done to prevent her from getting back her memory. Moving her things out of her apartment, having them crush her car. Having her go to those dumb sessions, and for what? Who would do those things? It didn't make sense!

The only thing that did make sense was that she needed to get as far away from Randy as she possibly could. She needed to get her baby and get away from that crazy man. It was clear that he didn't want a life with her that's why she was in the guest house. Latrease told herself, guest house because she was a guest, not a permanent resident. He must've felt guilty about knocking her up. That must've been why he let her stay there and paid her to work in his gym. He was never planning on telling her the truth. Latrease began to cry. A long much needed overdue cry.

The doctor had told her that she would need to take it easy for six weeks. She needed to get lots of rest and try not to do too much. Latrease decided she would act like she hadn't remembered a thing. She would take that time to heal and then she would move out and as far away from

Randy Jackson as she could. She'd saved quite a bit of money and remembered that she still had some left in a Credit Union in the city from her parents' life insurance policy.

The next day Latrease was asked if she'd come up with a name for the baby. "Yes I have, I would like to call her Keyana." She told the nurse. That day Latrease was visited by Randy's mom, Shemeka, and Bernard. They'd spent a couple hours talking to her and taking pictures of the baby. They brought flowers and cards and candy and Bertha had brought Latrease a new robe and gown and slippers to wear around the hospital.

She'd held Keyana in her arms and fed her milk from a bottle. The baby was precious and very adorable. Latrease had never been happier.

"When can you come home?" Kevin asked later that night.

"They say if there aren't any complications I can leave tomorrow."

Randy was sitting on the loveseat in the hospital room holding the baby. Latrease was so irritated she hadn't said a single word to him the whole day. Every time he'd say something to her she acted like she didn't hear him or she was too tired to respond.

Early the next morning a photographer was waiting to take the baby's picture. Latrease had put her on a pink dress that had ruffles at the end. She had brushed her hair and put a pink head band on her head. She had put cute little white socks with pink trim on her feet. The baby didn't smile for the picture but it was a pretty picture nevertheless.

After a few more hours Latrease and the baby were being released from the hospital.

"Are you hungry?" Randy asked after thirty minutes of silence in the car. Latrease was sitting in the back next to the baby. She hadn't said much to him in the last couple of days and he wondered why she'd been so quiet.

"Nope." She replied.

"It's a good thing they let you out today while the weather is nice, it rained all day yesterday." He told her.

"Oh."

"Are you sure you don't want to stop and get anything, we can go through the drive through at Boston Market if you like?"

"I said no, Randy! I am ok. I just wanna get home I still have to put her crib together."

"No you don't. Bernard and I finished that last night and we put the mobile up and sheets in the crib and the blanket and bumper pads too. You don't have to do anything but relax when you get there."

"How do you know I didn't want to do it Randy, and what happened to the privacy pact? Maybe, just maybe, I wanted to do this one thing for *MY* baby since you and your family and everybody else bought her all her things, may be I've been looking forward to this one thing! Now you have taking that away from me too!"

"Hey hey calm down, I'm sorry I

didn't think about it like that…"

"That's right you didn't think! I don't need you to go out of your way doing things for me because you feel obligated Dr Jackson. I can take care of myself!"

"I think we need to lay down some rules, for now on I will pay you rent for living in your guest house. In return I want my privacy. When I'm better I will get out of your hair for good. I say about two months, deal?"

Randy felt like he'd swallowed a golf ball. Where was all this coming from? Why was she so cranky and moody? Why did she want to move out?

"I met someone and he is really sweet, he asked me to move in with him and I think it would be a good thing for me and Keyana. I want to give her a home with two parents. He will be here to get us in two months."

Randy swerved into the other lane. He could not believe what he was hearing. It was all happening too fast for him. Was that why she'd been so distant the last few weeks? Had she started dating someone right under his nose? He didn't know what to do, what to say. He pulled over into a Wal-Mart parking lot. Then got out of the car and walked around and opened the door to where she was sitting.

His eyes were teary.

"Latrease I don't want you to leave. I need you."

"For what, Randy? What is it that you need me for?"

A couple pulled up beside them, got out and started walking towards the store.

"I just do, Latrease! You complete me!"

"What are you talking about Randy?" Latrease felt a tear slide down her cheek.

"Isn't this what you want? To get rid of me! You've done everything in your power to make sure I didn't remember that I was in love with you and you were not in love with me! You even got your child to lie!" She was crying now. "Well you don't have to worry about that anymore! I remember! It's all coming back to me now! I will get out of your life and you won't have to worry about me or *MY* daughter cramping your luxurious life anymore! I wish you would have just left me at that hospital in Valdosta!"

The baby started whining.

"Latrease you have it all wrong. I love you; I want to spend the rest of my life with you!"

He tried to grab her hand but she pushed him away.

"You sure have a hellova way of showing it!" she shot back.

"I'm sorry Latrease it's very complicated I had to lie..."

"I don't want to hear this Randy, can you please take us home or do I need to call a cab?"

"A cab, oh my God Latrease I am trying to be real with you, please let me explain."

He brushed the hair back from her face.

"Explain? Why don't you start by telling me what you did with all my stuff from my apartment?"

"It's in the shed next to the garden. Latrease I did this for us."

She opened the door to the car and grabbed the pacifier and put it in the baby's mouth.

"I have to be the dumbest girl in the world! I should have known something was up with you! No man does all this for a patient! Patient? I was never your patient! How could you do this to me Randy? Take me home please!"

Randy didn't know what to say or how to explain to her that he had good intentions with everything he'd done. He couldn't think. His stomach was in knots.

"I love you Latrease. The reason I did this was so you would not forget me forever. You had a condition. I'm sorry I ever hurt you. I need you in my life. I don't know what I would do if you were to leave me."

"What condition, what are you talking about Randy? Is this another lie?"

"No I promise. It's called AMD. The night you had the accident, you was mad at me. You thought I stood you up."

"Yeah that's because you did!" she snapped.

"I had every intention on being there. But as I was on my way I found out my son was in the hospital. I lost track of time."

"Hmmm"

"You were on the road and you were traumatized. Your mind went into overtime and it came up with a way for you to suppress the thing that made you so mad. That was me. I'm sorry about all of this Latrease."

He sobbed. Tears raced off his face.

"How do I know you are telling the truth now?"

"There's only one person that knows about this and I know she would be willing to tell you, and that's Armentha."

"Your secretary?"

"Yes, she's known ever since it happened. I can call her now if you want me to."

"You don't have to do that. Let's get home it's getting late and I'm so tired. This is all so much for me to take in right now. I need some time to think." Latrease sat down in the car next to the baby.

"She's so precious Randy; we made a beautiful little girl." She smiled.

"I know."

***

Exactly six weeks later, Latrease lay in her bed. She'd had a long day. Keyana had gone to the doctor for her six week check up. She'd gotten her second set of immunizations and had been a bit feverish earlier. Now she was sound asleep in the nursery.

Latrease tossed and turned as she dreamed of a man. A black man. A black man lying next to her. A black man lying next to her in a bed that wasn't strange anymore. A black man lying next to her in a room she'd decorated. A bed she and her husband now shared. She could see him so clear. He was laying there next to her, holding her. She loved holding him.

He was more than just the man of her dreams. He was her companion. He was her soul mate. She heard the faint sound of Keyana whining in the background. Randy got up to check on her and returned to bed a few minutes later. Latrease held her eyes closed pretending to be sleep. Randy kissed her eyelids softly. She smiled. His kisses were tender, delicate. He kissed her ears, her neck, and then her lips.

He held and caressed her as he kissed her shoulders, her breast and slowly made his way down to her belly. He twirled her belly button with his tongue and then continued his journey south of her equator.

"Mmm", he whispered as he licked the outside of her panties. He'd waited so long for this moment. It had been six hours since they made their vows in front of family, and friends. She was sexier than ever! He kissed her thighs slowly spreading them apart. She whimpered as he slid himself inside. She was as hot as fire. He loved the way her juices flowed over his erection. He held her face as he kissed her lips. Their tongues danced the tango as they made love over and over and over again that night, their honeymoon night, in their bed.